SO-BNJ-865

Sins

of the

Father

A Rose Gardner Mystery Novella

Books by Denise Grover Swank

Rose Gardner Mysteries
Twenty-Eight and a Half Wishes
Twenty-Nine and a Half Reasons
Thirty and a Half Excuses
Falling to Pieces (novella)
Thirty-One and a Half Regrets
Thirty-Two and a Half Complications
Picking Up the Pieces (novella)
Thirty-Three and a Half Shenanigans
Rose and Helena Save Christmas (novella)
Ripple of Secrets (novella)
Thirty-Four and a Half Predicaments
Thirty-Four and a Half Predicaments Bonus Chapters (ebook only)
Thirty-Five and a Half Conspiracies
Thirty-Six and a Half Motives
Sins of the Father (novella)

Rose Gardner Investigations
Family Jewels

Magnolia Steele Mystery
Center Stage
Act Two

The Wedding Pact Series
The Substitute
The Player
The Gambler
The Valentine (short story)

Bachelor Brotherhood Series
Only You
Until You (May 2016)

Sins

of the

Father

A Rose Gardner Mystery Novella

Denise Grover Swank

This book is a work of fiction. References to real people, events, establishments, organizations, or locations are intended only to provide a sense of authenticity, and are used fictitiously. All other characters, and all incidents and dialogue, are drawn from the author's imagination and are not to be construed as real.

Copyright 2016 by Denise Grover Swank

Developmental Editor: Angela Polidoro
Copy edit: Shannon Page
Proofreader: Carolina Valdez Schneider
All rights reserved.

Part One

Chapter One

Rose

"H ave you heard the news?"

I stopped fishing around in my purse and looked up at Brittany, the chattiest waitress Merilee's Café has ever known. I'd long since tuned her out. "Sorry?"

She repeated her question as I handed her a twenty-dollar bill to pay for the lunch I was picking up for myself and my best friend, Neely Kate. We were stuck working in my landscaping office since we were behind in giving proposals on several jobs. After a few slow months, we were finally edging into prime landscaping season. I would have also gotten lunch for Bruce Wayne, my RBW Landscaping business partner, but it was a warm and sunny early May afternoon and he was out with his crew.

Even though I had no idea what Brittany was talking about, she was prone to hurtful gossip. I wasn't sure I should encourage her. "What news?"

"About Joe Simmons."

I tried not to gasp. I'd heard some things—none of them great—but I refused to gossip about him. He may have been my ex-boyfriend, but he was also my business partner in Gardner Sisters Nursery, and we'd tried very hard to be friends. I still cared about him. I couldn't deny that I was beyond curious about what she might know, but I wasn't going to ask. "No. I haven't heard a thing."

She leaned closer and whispered, "He's back in town."

"Really?" I couldn't help sounding hopeful. The last time I'd seen him was at the hospital in February, a few days after everything had gone down—and I do mean *everything.* In the space of a day, we'd found out that Neely Kate was Joe's illegitimate half-sister, Joe's pregnant ex-girlfriend Hilary and their unborn baby had been killed by Joe's father, Joe's sister Kate had shown us all that she was truly crazy, and Joe had killed his father to save me. Then, while we were both in the hospital recovering from our wounds, my boyfriend Mason had broken up with me.

My life had been forever altered that day, but Joe's life had been shattered to pieces.

Yet Brittany forged on, oblivious to my inner turmoil as she handed me my change. "I heard that he's been at his farmhouse for a week. Only, nobody knew because he's lying low. Probably hiding in shame."

That spiked my anger. "Shame?" I asked, snatching my bag out of her hand. "What on earth does that man have to be ashamed of?"

My tone caught her by surprise. "His father. His sister."

I almost asked which sister, but as far as I knew, no one in town had discovered Neely Kate's secret. "Joe's father made his own choices, and so did his sister. In case you hadn't noticed, people have free will. Their behavior was out of his control."

Her eyes narrowed and she spoke in a haughty tone. "Are you sure about that? From what I heard, Joe's father was a bad man hiding behind fancy suits and a lot of money. Turns out he had criminal ties to a lot of businesses in southern Arkansas. Plus, he financed Joe's campaign for state senator last fall. Sure, Joe was the chief deputy sheriff, but how do we know he wasn't as corrupt as his dad? Maybe he was only working for the sheriff's department to clean up his father's messes."

"I know Joe Simmons. He would never be part of any of that."

She gave me a look that told me how much she pitied my naïveté. "I wonder why he came back. Surely he's not getting his job back."

I shook my head in disbelief. "Why on earth wouldn't he get his job back? He didn't do anything wrong!"

She put a hand on her hip. "I'm not surprised you'd take his side. I heard that you were hooking up with Skeeter Malcolm, a known criminal, behind your boyfriend's back. No wonder poor Mason Deveraux left town. How embarrassing would it be for the district attorney to find out his girlfriend is sleeping with the enemy?"

I considered protesting her false allegations, but I knew it would be wasted breath.

I heard a racket to my left and noticed that a woman had dropped her beverage, the broken glass pieces having scattered across the floor. She and everyone else watched us with rapt attention.

Spinning around, I stomped toward the door. A man in a business suit scampered out of my way as I reached the door and flung it open. The little bell attached to the doorknob swung wildly, but I didn't bother trying to fix it before the door slammed shut behind me. Merilee's was right across the square from my business, and the food was delicious, but between the many memories of Mason and the rude waitress, maybe it was time to find a new place to get lunch.

I tore across the square and didn't stop until I entered my office.

My dog Muffy jumped up from her dog bed under my desk and greeted me at the front door with a wagging tail. Her back end rumbled, and I waved my hand in front of my face, staving off the noxious cloud with an irritated groan.

"Jeez, Muffy. Did you eat a case of beans this morning?"

Neely Kate turned from her computer screen and quirked an eyebrow. I was rarely harsh with Muffy, even if she did smell like rotten eggs more often than any of us would have liked.

I set the food bag down on her desk, then bent down and rubbed Muffy's head. "I think we're going to have to start getting our lunch somewhere else."

Neely Kate's eyes widened in surprise as she removed a takeout container and opened the lid. "Why? What happened?"

"I knew Brittany was a gossip, but I had no idea she would be so mean to my face."

Neely Kate slapped the container down on her desk, looking madder than if Miss Mildred had been dumped into the Wagon Wheel bar on Ladies' Night. "What did she say?"

I considered not telling her. I really didn't want to repeat it, but now that I'd brought it up, I knew Neely Kate wouldn't let it rest until I told her what I knew. "She blamed me for running Mason out of town." My voice broke, which only fueled my anger. I'd finally gotten to a place where I wasn't sad all the time.

"She said *what*?"

"She says he left because I embarrassed him."

"Because you were the Lady in Black?" she asked in surprise. "They put it together?"

I cringed. While a few people knew about the alter ego I'd created to help James Malcolm (Skeeter to almost everyone else) from time to time, it wasn't exactly common knowledge. "I don't think so, but she

9

said everyone thinks I was sleeping with James." I paused to take a breath. "Does everyone really think that, Neely Kate? I need you to be straight with me."

Neely Kate had an uncanny way of knowing what was going on in the county, but unlike Brittany, she rarely shared what she knew and never used it to hurt anyone. "Your name was tied to him in the news twice, Rose," she said, reaching for my hand and squeezing it. "You have to know that people were wondering why he'd give two figs about you."

"You mean the two times Joe's dad tried to kill me?" I couldn't deny that James had been there to protect me in both instances. While it had made the news, I hadn't heard a single rumor. Then again, I guess you don't usually hear the rumors when you're the subject of them.

"You know people were wondering why he was with you. But only a few people talked about it, and I haven't heard anything in over a month. Most of the talk was after people found out Mason was back in Little Rock. It's all died down since then."

I took my food and sat down at my desk, pushing out a sigh. "Well, Brittany's talking about it now."

"No one else is. And you haven't seen Skeeter in over a month."

I didn't comment on that. Truth was James and I had been getting together once a week at our old meeting spot behind the deserted Sinclair gas station for a couple of months now, with the exception of the week I'd spent in Houston to donate bone marrow for my sister. James and I had become friends. Our Tuesday night meetings were often the highlight of my week, and I wasn't about to let a bunch of busybodies with loose tongues ruin it.

"She specifically brought up Mason leaving?" Neely Kate asked. When I nodded, she rolled her eyes. "It was no secret that she had a huge crush on him, and she wasn't happy when she found out you'd snatched him up. She's stupid enough to think she had a chance with him." She shook her head in disgust. "*As if.* I hope you had a vision of her and told her something terrible. Like that she'd spent hours waiting on customers with spinach in her teeth."

"I wish I'd been quick enough to think that fast."

She shot me an ornery grin. "Sometimes your gift is wasted on you."

Gift. I used to consider my visions a curse, but there was no denying they had saved plenty of lives since I'd started purposely using them instead of letting them happen spontaneously.

"Have you had any visions yet today?" she asked.

"No." I often saw things in my visions that were none of my business, which made another aspect of my talent—spontaneously blurting out whatever I'd seen—particularly awkward. Trial and error had taught me that if I forced visions, I'd have fewer unplanned ones, so I'd been trying to force small visions with my friends, looking for benign things in the near future. Sometimes even those ended badly. Like when I saw Neely Kate plucking a hair from her mole or Jonah sitting on the toilet after he'd had a bad batch of tacos at the new Mexican restaurant.

"It's not too late to run across the street and have one now. I bet you could see her doing the horizontal mambo with Anita Stanford's husband."

I cringed. "I think I'll pass." I opened my container, grabbed a piece of chicken from my salad, and gave it to Muffy as a peace offering. "But that wasn't all. I'm sure she was up to something." I stabbed a piece of lettuce with a plastic fork. "She dropped a piece of bait, hoping I'd give her more information."

"About what?"

"Joe."

Neely Kate's face paled. "What about him?"

"She said he's back in town. That he's been out at his rented farmhouse for the last week."

Pain filled her eyes, and she turned back to the computer.

"He's been through a lot, Neely Kate."

"Yeah. I know."

She'd found out they were half-siblings hours before the big showdown in the abandoned factory, where Kate had brought me, Joe, Hilary, J.R., Mason, James, and even Neely Kate together to seek revenge on her father. In all the craziness, Kate had told Joe that Neely Kate was their half-sister, and he'd never really acknowledged it. After the dust had settled, Joe had left town without a single word to Neely Kate.

She had been hurt beyond belief.

Until now, the only thing we'd known about Joe was from the sheriff's official statement: Chief Deputy Joe Simmons was taking a leave of absence of indeterminate length to deal with personal issues. We'd had no idea when or if he was coming back. Every single text and phone call I'd made to him had gone unanswered.

"I'm sure he just needs more time," I said.

Neely Kate started to pound on the keyboard as though trying to beat it into submission before she said, still typing furiously, "Why would I care? You know we bickered like cats and dogs after you two broke up. This doesn't change a thing."

"Neely Kate . . ."

She turned to me, her eyes a mixture of anger and pain. "Let it go, Rose."

"But—"

"Let it go." The coldness in her voice caught me by surprise.

Muffy sat at my feet and let out a low whine. I leaned over to rub her head. Time to change the subject. "After I finish lunch, I need to go to a job site and look something over with Bruce Wayne. Wanna come?"

"No."

I gave her a long stare, and after a good minute of ignoring me, she spun her chair to face me full on. "Rose, I know you're trying to make me feel better, but Joe made his choice. I never expected anything from him at all, so whatever. His loss."

I didn't believe that for a minute. Truth be told, I was bitterly disappointed with him myself, but I also felt compelled to give him a break. He'd watched his father kill his pregnant ex-girlfriend, then killed his father to save me. That would mess anyone up. I couldn't blame him for needing time to deal with it all. But my heart was breaking for my best friend.

I had to figure out a way to fix this all. And I had a pretty good idea of where to start.

Chapter Two
Joe

God knew I'd burned plenty of bridges over the last ten years, but I was pretty damn sure I'd burned the last few I had left.

I could kiss any hope of a relationship with Neely Kate goodbye.

She had reached out to me—multiple times—and I'd ignored her on pretty much every medium that existed. When I first found out the truth, I'd been ashamed. I still was. But now my shame was for a different reason.

Neely Kate was my half-sister.

Three months after the discovery, I was still struggling to wrap my head around it. I'd known her for months and never once suspected. I tried to reassure myself with the knowledge that she hadn't known either. But looking back, I wondered if I *should* have suspected. She had my grandmother's blue eyes, my cousin's thick blond hair. Then there was the way we'd always bickered back and forth—like siblings—even before my breakup with Rose. And the fact that I'd always known that my father was a philanderer.

Common sense told me there was no way I could have known. For one, I had no idea about my father's involvement in Fenton County twenty-five years ago. And two, he'd always been so careful to make sure something like this never happened.

But my sister Kate had figured out the secret and gone to great lengths to prove it was true.

My mother hadn't seemed all that surprised by the news; nor did she seem to care. Her only concern was that Neely Kate would try to "get her grubby hands on our money." Then again, her immediate response to finding out about my father's death and Kate's arrest for kidnapping and attempted murder had been to hire a publicist. Her attempt to rewrite history to be more favorable to the Simmons family might have actually worked if the FBI hadn't become involved.

One of J.R. Simmons's precious Twelve had been arrested after the big showdown in the warehouse, and he turned state's evidence against his peers and my father. Once that happened, the rest began turning on each other and spilling the goods. Plenty of dirty deeds had been uncovered—a lot of them committed by my father. It was enough to make a man want to hang his head and hide away forever.

But Neely Kate and Rose weren't the only ones who'd reached out to me.

Two weeks after Hilary's funeral, Maeve Deveraux had showed up at my parents' front door in El Dorado.

My mother had been the one to answer the door. Under different circumstances, their meeting might have been humorous—Maeve with her quiet peace and confidence, and my mother clothed in her false outrage and smothered guilt.

"I can't believe you had the audacity to show up here unannounced!" my mother had shouted. "How dare you?"

"With all due respect, Mrs. Simmons," Maeve had said, her soft voice full of authority, "I'm here to see Joe. Not you. Will you please let him know that I'm here?"

But Maeve's serene dignity only pissed off my mother more. "Who do you think you are? You have no right to be here."

I stepped out of my father's office with a glass of whiskey in my hand, even though it wasn't yet noon. My heart flooded with relief when I saw the only mother figure to have shown me unconditional love and acceptance, even though I'd done nothing to deserve it. Especially from her. "Mother, the very fact you're so eager to throw her out on the street proves you know who she is, but I can see that you need a formal introduction." I stumbled into the foyer, ignoring the worry in Maeve's eyes. I gestured toward her. "Mother, this is Maeve Deveraux, mother to Savannah Deveraux, the mother of my first child—and the woman your husband paid to have viciously killed, along with my unborn baby."

Pain ripped through my chest, making it difficult to breathe. I took a gulp of my whiskey before continuing. "The woman your husband systematically destroyed even though she wasn't his designated target. No, Maeve Deveraux was just a casualty of war, collateral damage. And it wasn't enough that he had her daughter and grandchild murdered. No, my father had to toy with her son's life too."

Why was she here? I'd heard that Mason was taking a job in Little Rock. Was she here to blame me for that?

The sins of the father.

But I knew better. I knew her heart. I knew the worry and concern I'd find in her eyes when I looked into her face—which was exactly why I couldn't do it. I didn't deserve anything but censure from her, from anyone. I'd always suspected my father was up to no good, but I'd turned the other way. How many lives had he destroyed? How many times had he hurt this truly good woman, even if it was inadvertent?

"Joe." That one simple word—my name—held so much more compassion and love than my mother had ever given me.

But I still refused to look at Maeve. Gesturing toward my mother, I continued the introduction. "Maeve Devereux, this is Elizabeth Simmons, known as Betsy to her friends, but *really*, who are your friends when you're a great white shark swimming in shark-infested waters?"

"Joseph," my mother said in harsh rebuke.

18

I ignored her too. "She stood by while my father did terrible things. She claims innocence, but she had to know. If she knows every little piece of dirt on all her friends, then how could she not know the truth about her own husband?" I gestured wildly with my arms to demonstrate, spilling my drink on my hand. "Oops. You better get the maid, Mother. I think I spilled on your wool rug. Clean it up before it stains. How would that look?" I turned to look at her, my hatred growing. "God forbid there should be any sign of imperfection in this house. Especially in regards to your children. You've always been far more concerned about what people thought of me and Kate than our actual welfare."

"How can you say that?" she asked incredulously. "You're my children!"

I leaned closer, my hand tightening so hard around my glass it was a wonder it didn't shatter. "How many times have you been to see Kate since her arrest?" But then, I hadn't been to see her either. Not since she'd been moved to Little Rock.

Her eyes widened in surprise.

"How many times, Mom?"

She lifted her chin and gave me a look of defiance. "Your sister made her choice."

I shook my head. "No. You and Dad made it for her. Did he rape her too?"

My mother gasped, the blood draining from her face.

"Because I've thought about it. Only moments before my father shot Hilary, I found out that he'd raped her. She spent so much time here as a kid that she had to be like a daughter to him. So if he raped her, then why not Kate?"

"Joseph! Enough!"

I lifted the hand holding my drink, pointing to my temple with my index finger. "That would explain why Kate's as messed up as Hilary was." I released a derisive chuckle. "Not that we Simmons children need any more reason to be messed up."

Maeve took a step toward me. "Joe. Can we go somewhere to talk? Maybe get a cup of coffee?"

I pointed back to Maeve, still glaring at my mother. "Kate was going to kill her son, and who knows, maybe Hilary planned to do the same. Dad created a little army to sow his seeds of destruction."

"Joseph!" my mother shouted. "That's enough!"

"No. It's not *nearly* enough." I may have been the one to shoot and kill my father, but my intervention had come too late. The guilt of that hung around me like a noose, and I had a feeling it always would.

Realizing I was lost in a drunken stupor, my mother turned her anger on our guest. "You are not welcome here! Get out!"

Maeve held her ground. "And as I mentioned previously, Mrs. Simmons, I'm not here to see you. I'm here to see your son." I finally summoned the nerve to look at her. Her eyes were on me, and she looked like she wanted to pull me into a hug and take me far away. "Joe, please."

"I don't deserve your pity, Maeve. Give it to the people who deserve it."

"You can't stay here, Joe. This place is like poison to your soul. Come back with me."

I shook my head. "I can't come back. Nobody wants me in Henryetta."

Tears filled her eyes. "That's not true. You have so many friends and people who care about you."

"No. Not anymore."

"Rose cares about you. She's worried."

"Why?" I asked in disbelief. "How can she care about what happens to me after everything my father put her through? After everything Hilary and my sister did? After I arrested her and downplayed the danger she was in, all due to my father?"

"*You* are not responsible for the deeds of your father, Hilary, or even your sister."

"She was right to choose Mason over me. He's a righteous man. He had an amazing woman raise him, so how could he not be? Me?" My voice broke. "I'm nothing."

"Joseph!" my mother shouted. "Stop this right now. You're embarrassing yourself."

For a moment, Maeve looked like she was about to tell my mother off, but then she shook it off and took another step toward me. "Joe. You *are* a good man. A man with a good heart. You found your own way to that goodness, despite your upbringing."

I shook my head and, my voice breaking, said, "No. Rose did that."

"No." Maeve's tone brooked no argument. "She may have helped you discover another part of yourself, but it was there all along. When you and Savannah were together, you were good to her."

When we were together. Not after.

"Savannah." A new wave of guilt and anguish washed over me. I'd only known for a few weeks that my father had been behind her murder, intended to be a punishment to make me pay for straying from Hilary and the future he had planned for me. Every time I let myself think about it, it was just as painful as the first time I'd found out.

Maeve moved in front of me and clasped my face between her hands, giving me a smile full of love and acceptance. "You're a good person, Joe Simmons. You are *not* your father."

"No, you're not," my mother said in disgust. "But I wish to God you were. He wouldn't fall apart like this! You need to grow a backbone, Joseph. You need to be strong. It's up to you to carry on the family name. The family legacy."

"The family legacy? My father killed my family legacy. Twice!" I pulled away from Maeve and started to laugh, the uncontrollable laughter of a man who has lost everything. "You want me to be even *more* of a monster?" I asked in disbelief once I'd settled down enough to speak. "You want me to rape young girls and order murders and destroy people's lives?"

My mother looked like she would have strangled me if she could have gotten away with it. "Your father knew what he wanted. He had a purpose and a plan. He wasn't perfect, and he had his vices, but look at what he secured for our family—for you! You've got to pull yourself together and salvage what's left of it!"

I took a step back in horror. "I'm not taking over anything."

I couldn't believe what I was hearing. I'd told her that there was a good chance we were going to lose it all, but she refused to listen.

Mom's face reddened with anger. "It's your birthright."

"Fuck my birthright."

"Joseph!"

I wasn't sure if she was more upset over my pronouncement or my language. But Maeve stood to the side, watching it all. I had to make her go away, because looking at her was only a reminder of the man I'd pretended to be in Fenton County.

I turned to Maeve, filled with self-contempt. "You think I'm a good person, but I'm not. Not even close. I killed my father. I shot him twice. I wanted to be sure he was good and dead. I couldn't risk him surviving the first shot so he could destroy more lives."

Maeve looked close to tears. "I'm sure that was hard."

I shook my head. "No. It wasn't. Pulling that trigger wasn't hard at all. It felt good. Like I was cleansing the world of a demon." I stared into her confused face. "I have absolutely no remorse. Not one shred. If anything, I wish I'd shot and killed him a year ago. Before he got his claws in Savannah."

"Joe, you didn't know."

"No. But I should have. I should have seen him for the monster he truly was." I paused and pointed to my chest. "And now I'm a monster too, because how could I kill a man, my own father, and feel nothing but relief?"

Maeve reached for me, but I took several steps backward, stumbling on the edge of the rug. "Go home, Maeve. Forget about me."

Her shoulders squared. "I will never forget about you. Do you hear me? I will *never* forget about you."

But her words faded as I went into my father's office and shut the door.

Surrounded by the echoes of a thousand evil deeds.

Chapter Three
Joe

The FBI arrived at my parents' front door on a cold and rainy day in late April.

And like a man waiting for his stroll to the gallows, I'd been expecting them.

I knew the seizure of my parents' property was a matter of when—not if—but I was still waiting to find out if charges would be filed against me as well. I'd been handling my father's business affairs after his death, but the campaign he'd waged the previous fall to get me elected state senator was riddled with questionable dealings. Over the years, my father had bribed and threatened a lot of people on my behalf, and I had a feeling that was going to bite me in the ass too.

After everything he'd done in my name, I deserved whatever happened to me.

When the lead investigator showed up at the door with a warrant, he took me to my father's office and shut the door. "Have a seat, Joe."

I stood in front of my father's massive desk and faced him, squaring my shoulders as I prepared for what he was about to tell me. "I'd rather stand."

He nodded, understanding filling his eyes. "I know it's an understatement to say I'm here under less than ideal circumstances, but there's some good news in all of this."

I gave him a blank stare.

"After examining all the evidence and taking into account how cooperative you've been during the investigation, we've decided not to press charges. We're convinced you had no knowledge of his illegal activities. While I doubt you'll ever be able to run for a political office again, you've been cleared of any wrongdoing. You're free to return to your chief deputy sheriff position."

I ran my hand over my head. "If they want me back."

"I know they put you on administrative leave while you were under investigation, but they've never given me or my agents any indication that you wouldn't be welcomed back. In fact, the sheriff called last week to check on the progress of your case. I'm pretty sure he's eager to get you back to work." He paused. "But there's bad news too," he continued. "In addition to your father's house, we've seized the other assets, including the bank accounts."

I nodded. That was no surprise either. I expected to feel pain or anxiety, but all I felt was a numbing relief. This was almost over.

The FBI agent continued, "You'll be followed by the stench of your father's actions for the rest of your life, but thankfully you've built a career in law enforcement that sets you apart from him. I suspect you'll be fine, especially if you decide to stay in Fenton County."

But did I want to go back to the sheriff's department? Did I want to go back to Fenton County at all? After everything my father, my sister, and Hilary had put Rose through, how could I face her? After ignoring Neely Kate for over two months, how could I face *her*?

But my father's money was gone. The house was gone. The only place I had to live was my condo in Little Rock and my rental house in Fenton County. I could try to return to the state police, but I'd burned bridges there too.

"Thanks for your honesty and cooperation, Joe," the investigator said. "I'm sorry you've had to go through all this."

"It's not exactly like I'm an innocent. I was a detective with the state police. I was a damned deputy sheriff. I should have seen all of this. I should have stopped him."

Compassion washed over his face. "We choose to see the best in our parents. It's hard to think they're capable of such atrocities."

That wasn't entirely true. While I had never suspected my father capable of murder—in fact, I'd insisted to Mason that he wasn't, which had put

Mason's life in greater danger—I had always known my father wasn't a good person. So why had I chosen to ignore all the signs? Because I'd found it inconceivable to see my father in that light, or because doing so would have meant turning my world on end?

I wasn't so sure it was the former.

Despite the FBI's claim that I wasn't complicit in my father's actions, I knew many people had suffered because I'd turned a blind eye.

"I wish you the best, Joe."

"Yeah, thanks," I said as I walked out of the office. My mother was in the foyer, irate and yelling at the agents streaming in through the front door.

"You can't just come into my home!" she shouted. "I have rights!"

"Actually, Mom," I said in a calm voice as I walked up to her, "they can."

She turned to me in panic and grabbed my arm, her nails digging into my skin. "Joseph! Do something!"

"What do you want me to do?"

"You have to stop them!"

"They have warrants. The judges Dad bribed are gone. This, Mother, is what justice looks like."

Her face paled and I could see that the gravity of the situation was finally sinking in. This wasn't something we could bribe our way out of. No publicist could fix this.

"What are they going to do?" she asked in a meek voice.

"They are taking your house. Your furniture. All your possessions. They have also seized your money. You have nothing. Absolutely nothing."

For the past two months, I'd warned her, yet she'd found the possibility preposterous. We were Simmonses, for God's sake. We were untouchable. But the Simmons reign was over.

A second wave of protest rose up. "You have to do *something*. Call our attorney."

"Mom. I told you last week that your attorney was arrested, and our new one says we're at the mercy of the government. It's over."

"But we have to do something," she repeated in panic.

"The only thing to do is leave."

She swallowed, her face turning gray. "Where will I go?"

I snorted. "I'd tell you to go stay with friends, but you don't exactly have any real friends, do you? I suppose that's a Simmons trait. We're too damned selfish to have real friends." But the desperation on her face softened my reaction. She truly had no idea what to do. "Go stay with your parents."

Horror filled her eyes. Her parents had done well for themselves, but nowhere close to the Simmons level of wealth, and my mother had never made an effort to hide her embarrassment about her parents and her upbringing. "What if they won't take me in?"

I released a bitter laugh. "Honestly, Mom. I really don't give a damn."

I left her in the foyer and found the poor frightened maid in the kitchen. She was wringing her hands, looking lost and uncertain, as an agent carried my father's computer out the back door.

"Mr. Simmons, they're taking things away."

"Mae, it's okay. They have a warrant."

She nodded, but she wrapped her arms across her chest as she watched another agent walk out the door.

"I'm sorry," I said gently, "but the government is seizing my parents' property, which unfortunately means that your services are no longer needed. My parents' money is gone, but I'll pay for the hours you've worked as well as a severance package. And I'll be happy to give you any references you need to find another job."

Tears filled her eyes. "Thank you, Mr. Simmons."

"Joe," I said, my chest tightening.

The reality of what was actually happening finally hit me full force, and I struggled to catch my breath. I knew I should feel relief or some sense of justice. My father—the man who had been so sure he was untouchable—was losing everything. But he wasn't here to face the pain and humiliation. Just like always, other people were picking up the pieces for him. "Mae, I need to leave the house for a short while, but I'll be back in less than an hour if you need help carrying your things to your car."

She shook her head in earnestness. "No need to do that, Mr. Joe. I'm more than capable of taking care of the few things I have here."

"I suggest you get packing right away. I'll tell the lead agent that your things aren't part of my father's estate."

I turned around to find the agent, but Mae called after me, "What will you do? Where will you go?"

"I don't know."

I left the house and found my car in the driveway. It had been excluded from the seizure because I'd bought it with my own money. Once I left the house, I drove on autopilot, not consciously deciding on a destination. Then I parked and walked the rest of the way, still acting on reflex.

That's how I found myself in the cemetery standing in front of Hilary's grave.

I could count on one hand the number of times I'd purposely come here, but I'd come countless times without planning to. My feelings for Hilary were complicated and messy, but my feelings for our baby were clear. I loved him.

The autopsy report told me I'd had a son.

When I reached Hilary's tombstone, I knelt in front of it, running my fingertips along the etchings. Her parents had spared no expense and had created a three-foot-tall monument with her name, birthdate, date of death, and the following epitaph: *Blessed daughter, loyal friend, loving mother*

I was sure the loyal friend line was a jab at me, although perhaps that was my own narcissism at work. There was no denying Hilary had been loyal to me, even if her devotion had warped her. Or more accurately, my father's abuse had warped her. When I visited her grave, I liked to think of her as the girl I grew up with. The happy, sweet girl who had won my heart, even if I had been too stupid to realize it. My father's yoke had chafed back then, and I'd rebelled. I couldn't help wondering how things would have turned out if I'd followed my heart instead. Would I have saved her from my father's abuse? With the advantage of hindsight, I knew when he'd started his molestation. How had I been too stupid, too self-centered to see it at the time?

"I'm sorry, Hil," I said, my voice breaking. "I failed you. And our baby too."

Two babies—and those were just my own—killed at the hands of my father. I couldn't help wondering if this was some sort of cosmic justice. Maybe I wasn't meant to have children at all, no matter how much I wanted them.

"It's not your fault," a woman said.

I jerked my head up and around, shocked to see Maeve standing behind me.

"How . . . ?"

She grimaced. "I stopped by the house to see you and found the commotion. The maid remembered me and told me you were probably at the cemetery."

"How did she know?"

"She said you come here whenever you seem upset. I have no idea how she knew. Maybe your mother?"

That explanation made sense. I wouldn't put it past my mother to have me followed.

I stood and shifted to the side of the grave so Maeve could stand next to me. "What are you doing here, Maeve?"

"I've come to take you home."

Releasing a bitter laugh, I turned my gaze to the headstones surrounding us. "I don't have a home. Everything's gone."

"No." I turned back to see her slowly shaking her head. "That's not true. Home isn't a place. It's the people who care about you." I started to protest, but she held up her hand. "You *do* have people who care about you. *I* care about you."

"Why?" I moaned. "Savannah would be alive if it wasn't for me." My father might have ordered her death, but I'd already left her and hurt her over and over again. Sure, I hadn't known about her pregnancy, but I'd ignored her pleas for help when she told me someone was stalking her. I was responsible for her death too. And our baby's.

"Joe." Maeve moved closer and put her hand on my arm. "Savannah loved you. Despite everything."

My chest felt tight with pressure, and I was dangerously close to losing it. "I've screwed up so much, made so many mistakes."

"I'm sure you've made mistakes, but so has everyone else. Rose is wallowing in guilt because she kept her Lady in Black secret from Mason. Mason's wallowing in guilt over walking away from her. I feel guilty for pushing Rose to keep her secret to save Mason. And Neely Kate . . ." She paused. "None of us are perfect, Joe. See? Not even me." She gave me a soft grin. "But living in guilt doesn't solve anything. It's selfish, when you stop and think about it."

"Selfish?"

"You're holding yourself back from the world, hiding the gifts you have to offer."

"Gifts?" I asked with a grunt. "I was given gifts— money, houses . . . Savannah. I threw them away. I lost everything, and it's my own damn fault."

"I'm not talking about the gifts that have been given to you. I'm talking about the gifts you have to offer other people."

I shook my head. "I don't have any."

"You do. The maid at your parents' house told me about your generous offer. The severance package. The reference. She wasn't your employee, yet you're making sure she's taken care of."

I snorted. "Don't act like I'm some damn saint. It's the decent thing to do."

She smiled, ignoring my statement. "Look at all the things you did around my house. The leaky faucet. The broken screen door. And you wouldn't accept a dime of repayment."

"You insisted on paying me with food. Besides, I owed you."

"No, Joe. You didn't owe me a thing." She was silent for a moment. "Why did you go into law enforcement?"

I snorted. "So I could help people. That's ironic, isn't it? I wanted to help people, but I just keep hurting them."

"Your father hurt so many more. And you stopped him. If you'd been following in his footsteps, you would have found a way to cover up what he'd done, but you held him accountable instead. You tried to make the world a better place by putting him behind bars."

"Like bars stopped him." I shook my head in disgust. "It never occurred to me that he'd escape from jail. How naïve was that?"

"Not naïve. You were trying to follow the law, something your father never respected."

"Fat lot of good it did. He still escaped."

"And you stopped him then too."

A memory flashed through my mind—the look on my father's face the second before I pulled the trigger. The shock. The fury.

"Too little, too late." It was a refrain that haunted my days, my dreams. Would probably haunt the rest of my life.

"Maybe, maybe not. You saved Rose's life."

"Another example of too little, too late. I broke up with her at my father's insistence and then ran right back to Hilary and got her pregnant. A decent man would have left Rose alone. But when I saw her at her nursery last October during that campaign stop, I realized I didn't want to live without her. I wouldn't leave her alone, even after I realized she was happier

35

with Mason." I pushed out a grunt of self-disgust. "My father had threatened her, and I was arrogant enough to think I could protect her. I thought I could use Dora's journal as leverage. I only put her in more danger." I looked down at the tombstone. "I should have walked away from her after I finished my undercover job. My father would have left her alone."

"I'm sure she thinks differently. She says you helped her become the person she is today."

I laughed. "No. She's a better person because she was smart enough to not take me back."

"Joe. Enough. You've made mistakes, but you've learned from them. It's time to come home."

"Come home? That's what I did after I killed my father. But now it's gone."

Her nose scrunched in disgust. "Your parents' house isn't your home. You came back here to settle your family crisis, and now it's done. There's nothing left for you to do here."

I glanced back at the tombstone. She was right. My work on my father's estate and businesses was at an end. But what did that mean for my future?

"*Joe.*"

I looked down into her warm and pleading eyes.

"It's time to let the past go. Come home and rebuild your life."

She was right. I had to go *somewhere*. Either my cold, sterile bachelor apartment in Little Rock, where I had no job and no real friends. Or back to my rented farmhouse outside of the Henryetta city limits, where I had slowly begun healing my heart by restoring the decades-old structure. Back to the few real friends I'd ever had. Would they welcome me?

"Neely Kate," I whispered. "I've hurt her."

"She's your family now. She'll get over it."

"I'm not so sure about that." Neely Kate was capable of holding grudges tighter than a squirrel hoarded nuts.

Maeve squeezed my forearm and smiled at me. "I guess you'll never know until you try. I never suspected you of being a coward, Joe Simmons."

I'd taken the coward's path more times than I could count. But here was the opportunity to change that. This was my chance to make things right.

I nodded, feeling an equal mixture of relief and anxiety. "Okay."

"Then let's go home."

After I went back to my parents' house, I grabbed the few things the FBI would let me take, made sure the maid escaped relatively unscathed, and then watched my mother's forlorn face in the backseat window of her father's car as he drove her away. Once it was all over, I got into my car and headed back to Fenton County.

Was I going home? It was time to figure that out.

Chapter Four

Rose

After lunch, Muffy followed me out the door and we climbed into the truck.

The morning had been cooler, but now fluffy clouds were building on the horizon, bringing humidity with them. I rolled down the windows and grinned as Muffy stuck her head outside and panted into the wind. I considered stopping by Joe's house first, but I had no idea how long I'd be there, and Bruce Wayne needed an answer from me about the landscaping job.

I spent the ten-minute drive trying to figure out how to cheer up Neely Kate. Her husband Ronnie was still missing, but she was moving forward with her divorce. She'd moved in with me at the farm, and even though both of us had been through life-changing breakups, we had found ways to move on. Mostly. But I could tell she felt abandoned, not just by Ronnie and Joe, but by her mother. Her mother had left her years ago, of course, but I knew Neely Kate had started hoping again after discovering the truth about her father. She'd let herself think her mother had taken off as a way to protect her, but nearly three months had passed since J.R.'s death, and her momma had made no attempt to reach out to her. It only made it worse that Joe's sister Kate had managed to get in touch with her momma to confirm that J.R. was her father.

I had no idea how to fill that void created by all her losses.

Pride flooded my chest when I pulled up to the curb in front of the house Bruce Wayne and his crew were working on. As I watched my friend and business partner talking to one of the men in his crew, I marveled at how the beaten-down man I'd met in the courthouse ten months before had blossomed into this confident leader of a four-man crew.

I hopped out and Muffy followed, immediately taking off toward the group of men. A broad smile spread across Bruce Wayne's face as my little dog jumped up on his legs. He pulled off his gloves and then bent down to pick her up, rubbing the back of her head.

"It's looking good," I said, stuffing my hands into my jeans pockets. "You guys are making great progress."

"Yeah. We're wrapping up the removal of the front bushes sooner than expected, but now that most of them are out, I think we need to alter the height of the wall. The bad news is that it's going to increase the amount of stone we need as well as the labor."

After going over the design, I agreed and we decided I'd be the one to call the homeowners.

He looked over at his crew. "Our business is doing pretty good, ain't it?"

"Much better than I dreamed when we decided to do this crazy thing last November. We were in the black last month." I studied the crew myself, amazed by how far we'd come. "I'm glad we took a chance."

"Anna says life ain't worth livin' if you ain't takin' chances."

I beamed. "Anna, huh?"

He laughed. "Truth be told, I learned that lesson from you last fall when you suggested workin' with Skeeter Malcolm, but Anna keeps the screws on me. When I start falling back into my hermit hole, she makes me get out and do things." He paused. "I have some news."

"Oh yeah?" I asked with interest.

"We're moving in together. David moved in with his girlfriend, and my lease is up. Anna's lease is up next month, so we're gonna look for a place together."

"That's wonderful! I'm so happy for you!"

I'd gotten to know Anna better over the last few months. She worked at the nursery Joe and I co-owned, and she'd really stepped up after my sister Violet, also a co-owner, had needed to make her unexpected long-term trip to Houston. I had no idea what we would have done if Anna and Maeve hadn't been so eager to help.

"How are you doin'?" he asked quietly, and I knew that he was referring to my breakup with Mason. "I keep meanin' to ask you, but it's . . ."

"Awkward?" I forced a grin. "I'm hanging in there." When he remained silent, I added, "I'm fine. Really."

"Maybe it's time for you to move on. Look for someone else."

I shook my head, surprised I was having this conversation with him of all people, but Bruce Wayne was one of the few people I could be honest with. With him, I never felt the need to pretend. "I moved on too fast after I broke up with Joe. Maybe if I'd given myself some time, Mason and I would have worked."

"You really believe that?" he asked, sounding skeptical.

"Honestly? I'm not sure. But I have to believe that Mason was right. I need to spend more time on my own, figuring out who I am now and what I want. Because if I don't, then our breakup feels . . . purposeless." A lump filled my throat.

To my surprise, he put an arm around my back and pulled my head to his shoulder. "You are one of the strongest people I know, Rose Gardner. Nothing you've done is purposeless, but don't spend your life waiting for Mason to come back. Part of living is doin', and I'm pretty sure that includes dating."

I laughed and wiped a stray tear from my cheek. "Let me guess—more wisdom from Anna?"

"She's a pretty smart woman. I have no idea why she puts up with the likes of me."

I pulled back, ready to chastise him for belittling himself, but then I saw his wide grin. I smacked his arm, shaking my head. "I don't know what to do with you."

His grin spread. "Well, we've got a lot of years to figure it out, since it looks like we'll be working together for a long time."

I laughed and glanced around, looking for Muffy. She usually stayed close, so I got worried when I didn't see her. "Where's Muffy?"

Bruce Wayne glanced around the job site. When he didn't see her, his back stiffened and he asked one of his men something in Spanish. The man shrugged and went back to work, but Bruce Wayne rushed over to the road, scanning the area.

I was about to panic when I heard her bark in the next-door neighbor's yard.

"Muffy!" I called out as I walked over. She was in the bushes by the neighbor's front porch, cuddled up to a white-and-black dog only slightly bigger than her.

The front door flew open and a woman with a baby on her hip walked out. Her mouth dropped in surprise. "Rose?"

I gasped when I realized she was my old next-door neighbor. She'd had the baby around the time I'd left Momma's old house, and she'd been desperate to move somewhere bigger. "Oh, my word! Heidi Joy! Is that *Clementine*?"

She pushed the door open, hurried down the steps, and threw one arm around me, squishing her baby between us. "I can't believe it!" she gushed. "And yes, this is Princess Clementine. The boys spoil her rotten, hence the name. She's six months old now and bigger than the boys were at her age." She looked around. "What are you doing here?"

"We're doing the landscaping next door."

She leaned to the side for a look, then turned back to me. "I had no idea the neighbors were having landscaping done. Y'all have made quick progress."

I smiled. "RBW Landscaping is growing by leaps and bounds. Bruce Wayne has a crew now, and they get things done."

"That's amazing, especially since you just started with that church last fall."

"Miss Rose?" a little boy squealed as he ran down the steps. "Did Muffy come for a playdate with Hugo?"

"Tommy!" I exclaimed. "I can't believe how big you've gotten. Who's Hugo?"

Heidi Joy waved her hand toward the dog who was currently sniffing Muffy's butt. "Rose, meet Hugo. The boys missed Muffy so much, and since we own this house instead of renting and have a big backyard, Andy and I decided to let them have a dog. We got Hugo from the animal shelter."

"That's wonderful," I said. "He and Muffy seem to be friends." She was bouncing around him, her tail wagging furiously as he ran in circles around her. "He has a lot of energy."

Heidi Joy sighed. "He sure does. He digs holes around the fence and keeps getting out. We're lucky he hasn't run off."

The baby in her arms studied me like I was an alien, but then a big smile lit up her face.

"Can I hold Clementine?" I asked.

"Of course!"

My heart melted as I reached out for the butterball of a baby. Her smile fell and she studied my face with a serious expression as I settled her on my hip. "How's Andy? How are the boys?"

We chatted for a few minutes, catching up on our lives, though I only shared the safe and easy side of my story. When I glanced back at Bruce Wayne and his crew, they were starting to unwrap the ties around the stacks of stone that sat on a pallet on our client's driveway. Which meant they were waiting for permission to get started on the wall. "It's been great seeing you, Heidi Joy, but I need to get back to work."

Her smile faded and she reached for the baby. "I heard about Violet. How's she doing?"

After I handed back the baby, I absently rubbed one of the incision scars on my lower back. "So far, so good. She had her bone marrow transplant, and if she keeps doing well, she can probably come home in another month or so."

"I heard you were the one who donated."

"We were lucky I was a match," I said, then turned to see Bruce Wayne waiting. "I've got to go. Let's try to meet for coffee sometime. I'd love to catch up more."

"Sounds great. Just be sure to come by when Andy Jr.'s home and bring Muffy with you. You know he loves that little dog."

I started to say, "Will do," but my head began to tingle and my vision faded at the edges, the telltale sign of an impending vision.

As it took hold, the sunny afternoon disappeared and the sky went dark. A gust of wind nearly blew me over.

"Hugo!" I shouted in a tiny voice that was lost in the wind. I recognized the voice as Tommy's—I was seeing this vision through his eyes.

"Where'd he go?" another boy asked.

"He took off running," I said in Tommy's voice. Then something whacked me in the back of the head.

"I told you to be more careful! Hugo's afraid of storms!"

I heard Heidi Joy shouting as the boy next to me ran down the street. "Andy Jr.! You come back here right now!"

The stormy afternoon disappeared, returning me to the sunny present, and I blurted out, "Hugo's going to run off in the storm."

"What?" Heidi Joy asked in confusion.

Most people didn't know about my visions, and I liked to keep it that way. But sometimes explaining them was difficult. "What I meant is that it looks like a storm's building to the west, and Hugo seems like such a live wire, I suspect he might run off." Then I hastily added, "Muffy used to." Which was totally untrue. I could only think of one time Muffy had run off, and that was right after I'd first gotten her nearly a year ago.

"Oh," she said, shifting Clementine. "You're probably right. I'll keep an eye on him."

I leaned forward and caught Tommy's attention. "You too, okay?"

He nodded, his serious little eyes pinned on mine.

I waved goodbye and called to Muffy to follow me as I pulled out my phone. Another glance to the west proved a storm was building, which meant I needed to take care of this phone call and pay a visit to Joe before all hell broke loose.

Part Two

Chapter Five
Joe

It caught me by surprise how right this place felt. The Fenton County farmhouse I'd rented last November had been a disaster when I returned from El Dorado. I'd started repairing and remodeling as soon as I moved in, but when rumors surfaced that Skeeter Malcolm had taken over the crime world, I'd started to put in a lot more overtime at work. Especially when it looked like a new player had joined the pack—a woman who dressed to the nines but always wore a veil. She went by the mysterious name the Lady in Black.

Mason Deveraux and I had spent a lot of time trying to figure her out—where she was from, her motives, and what she was after. Neither of us ever would have guessed the Lady in Black was Rose in disguise. In fact, I suspect that if someone had asked the pair of us to bet our lives on it, we'd both be dead.

But soon after Lady's appearance, Mason's life had been threatened and my father had begun showing interest in Fenton County, a location he'd always claimed to despise; and then there was Hilary's pregnancy. Any free time I'd previously had to work on the house pretty much evaporated.

Now, I'd been back in Fenton County for nearly a week, doing nothing but working on the place, sitting on the front porch drinking beer, and feeling a peace I'd never experienced. I was still haunted by demons— they nipped at my heels and screamed in my head—but I was finding more and more pockets of quiet. For the first time, I thought maybe, just maybe, I might be okay.

I took a break from installing sheetrock in the living room and went into the kitchen to grab a beer. As I opened the fridge, I heard a knock at the front door.

"It's open," I called out, grabbing another beer with it. "I picked up something at the store that I think you'll like." I'd discovered Maeve liked light beer, so I'd picked up a six-pack on my supply run to Columbia County the day before. I figured Columbia County was safe. No one knew me up there, and that was the way I preferred it. I was working my way back to society.

I rounded the corner into the living room and promptly stopped in my tracks, blinking in surprise. It wasn't Maeve standing in the threshold. It was Rose and Muffy.

Rose was wearing a pair of faded jeans and a dark blue T-shirt that scooped low enough to show the rise of her breasts. Her hair was pulled back into a ponytail, and I noticed she had let it grow longer over the last few months. She wore little makeup, but then she'd never worn much. She didn't need it. A more natural look suited her.

I continued to stare at her in disbelief as Muffy tackled me, jumping up on my legs and barking in excitement. I shook my head and tried to clear it. "Sorry. I thought you were Maeve."

Guilt washed over her face, and she took a step back. "I'm sorry. I can go . . ."

"No." My voice was tight. "Don't." Seeing her brought a mixture of relief and guilt and more of that feeling of being at home, but that shouldn't have surprised me. Rose had been the first person to show me what a home really was. "Please stay."

A soft smile lit up her eyes, but there was a sadness there that I'd only seen after our breakup. Until she'd found happiness with Mason. "So it really is true," she said softly. "You're back."

My breath stuck in my throat. "People know?"

"I suspect not many. Neely Kate didn't know, and she usually knows everything." She cringed as soon as her best friend's name left her mouth.

I ignored the mention of my half-sister. "Did Maeve tell you?" I asked, even though it seemed unlikely as Maeve had promised to keep it quiet.

While I knew Maeve worked at the nursery, I had no idea if the breakup had put a strain on her relationship with Rose.

Rose shook her head. "No."

Muffy continued to bark, and I bent down and scooped her up, juggling the unopened beers with one hand. "I was about to sit on the porch and drink a beer. I thought you might be Maeve, so I grabbed one for her. You're welcome to it." I held the bottles toward her.

I could see the wheels spinning in her head. Her hesitation. Was she about to chastise me for drinking at two o'clock in the afternoon? Or did she plan to rip me to shreds for being gone so long without a word?

But her small smile returned as she grabbed the light beer I'd gotten for Maeve, and then she spun around and headed out the front door.

I followed and we sat in the two lawn chairs on the porch. The chairs were a constant fixture, because I found peace sitting by myself and surveying the fields in front of the house. I had bought the second chair for Maeve since she usually came every day around dinnertime to check on me and bring me food. She'd tried to convince me that I could hear the answers to all my questions if I listened to the rustling crops closely enough. So far I'd only heard geese flying home for the winter and cars on the highway, which ran several hundred feet from my front door.

I set Muffy on the floor next to me before I reached over and twisted off the cap to Rose's beer, then my own, and tossed the metal lids on the small cast iron table between us. Muffy put her paws on my legs, and I leaned over and rubbed her head while we sipped our beers in silence.

"I've been worried about you," she finally said.

I almost told her that I was fine, but I didn't see the point in lying. She knew I'd been a mess and still was.

"I heard the FBI took your parents' house."

I lifted the bottle to my mouth and hesitated before I took another sip. "It's true."

"I'm sorry, Joe."

"I'm not."

She turned to me, all wide-eyed shock.

"The Simmons empire was built on blood money. I don't want any of it. Well, that's not entirely true. I want enough to take care of Kate, but nothing for me."

I expected her to cringe or show fear or anger—something at the mention of my sister—but all she did was ask, "How's Kate doing?"

"They finally deemed her mentally incompetent to stand trial. She's in a psych ward in Little Rock."

"I know you and Kate never really got along, but it has to be hard for you to see her like that."

"I haven't since she was committed a month ago." I lifted a shoulder into a half-shrug. "That's not exactly true. I've been to the facility. I just haven't seen *her*."

"Does she not want to see you?"

I took a sip to stall. "I'm not sure. I'm too ashamed to face her."

"Joe."

The sympathy in her voice sliced through my heart. My pain poured out, suffocating me with grief.

"Don't," I choked out. "Don't feel sorry for me. I'm the least scathed person in this whole mess."

"That's not true, Joe. You lost *so much*."

"And yet here I sit. In one piece. I have my home, even if it's rented, and apparently I still have my job."

"Stop." There was an authoritative tone to her voice that I wasn't used to hearing from her. I recognized it as the same tone she'd used to confront my father. When she'd worn her hat and veil as the Lady in Black.

That woman intrigued me. Where had she come from? She'd probably been there all along, but I'd never once seen a hint of it. Further proof I wasn't the man for her. Mason had encouraged that strength to blossom, while I'd tried to stunt it.

A soft, sad smile lifted her mouth as she stared out into the fields. "Remember when we sat on my front porch last June and you taught me the rules of drinking?"

That night was forever etched into my brain. When I was old and senile and couldn't remember my own name, I was sure I'd remember that night. But I kept my feelings to myself and gave her my own sad smile. "Yeah."

"That seems like ages ago, but it hasn't even been a year. So much has changed." She turned to face me, looking nothing like the girl I'd failed to resist that night. That girl had been innocent yet so eager to explore the great big world that had just opened up for her. The woman sitting next to me looked worn and battle weary.

"Yeah."

She kept her gaze on me. "You told me that you wanted to be Joe McAllister, the man I fell in love with, but you also claimed he was a façade. That the real you would have come out in the end."

I shook my head. "Rose, stop." I didn't want to be reminded of everything I'd lost.

"I've always told you that you *are* that man. You could be him."

"And I proved you wrong."

It was her turn to shake her head. "No, Joe. That man is in you. You just have to *be* him." She turned her body to face me, a fire lighting her eyes. "You were so scared those first few months we were together, so scared your family would come to claim you and you'd lose the life you wanted."

"And I *did* lose it," I said, my agony growing. "Why are you rubbing this in my face? Is this your way of making me pay? For taking Mason from you? For sabotaging your life?"

"Taking Mason from me?" she asked in disbelief. "No one took him from me. I lost him all on my own, with my lies and deceptions. I hid my secret life from him, and from you and from everyone else, but you want to know *my* shame, Joe?" Her voice was shaking. "I'm not sorry I did it. Maybe I would change a few things if I could, but I wouldn't change becoming the Lady in Black." She looked up into my face, her eyes bright. "I saved Mason several times over. I saved you. I can't be sorry for that. No matter what it cost me."

Though she spoke with confidence, I could see she was holding something back, some secret she still wasn't willing to share.

"Joe, listen to me." She set her bottle on the table and took my hand. "Your family can't hurt you anymore. You're free. You can be anyone or anything you want to be. You can become Joe McAllister, and no one's going to stop you. Not Hilary. Not your father. Not Kate."

I struggled to catch my breath as the truth washed over me.

"When Mason left, my heart broke into a million pieces, but he knew I needed the chance to be free. No expectations from anyone. No one holding me back. I could just be me."

"You wanted that?" I asked. "Freedom?"

"No. Not at the time, and I still feel like a part of me is gone, but he was right to leave. Sometimes we have to walk through fire, then rise from the ashes and see who we've become. That's what I'm doing right now. I'm seeing the person I'm supposed to be. And this is *your* chance to be the man you always *wanted* to be."

I hadn't considered that before now, but she was right. I had been freed from my family's interference. Forever. "And the pain?"

Her hand squeezed tighter. "It hurts like hell, but I'm finding my way to the other side, and so will you."

"What if this is as good as it gets, Rose?" I asked. "What if I should just give up?"

There was a flicker of fear in her eyes before they became firm again. "Life's not done with you yet, Joe McAllister."

My throat burned and I choked back a sob. "I don't think I can do it, Rose."

She got out of her chair and kneeled at my feet, taking both of my hands in hers. "You can. You have friends who care about you. Me. Maeve." She paused. "Neely Kate."

I tried to jerk free, but she held on tight.

"I have no idea what you're thinking, Joe, but Neely Kate needs you just as much as you need her, even if you don't realize it."

I shook my head, unable to speak as tears burned my eyes.

"I know she's not your full sister, but look at Violet and me. Sure, we've had our differences, but I'd do anything for her, and she protected me time and time again growing up. And I know the situation is different for you and Neely Kate. I'm sure it's hard to accept her when she's the hard evidence that your father cheated on your mother. But if you can overlook that and get over the shame that she's your sister—"

"Shame?" I asked in shock. "Why would I be ashamed she's my sister?"

She grimaced. "Because . . ."

"Because she's a bastard?" I asked, sounding harsher than intended. "I *am* ashamed, Rose, but not for the reason you think." I got up and stood in front of the railing, staring out into the coming storm. "God, no. Neely Kate's the victim in all of this."

She rose to her feet as well but didn't move from in front of the chair. "Then why on earth have you shut her out?"

"My father. The destruction he left in his wake. Literally everything he touched was scorched by his greed and his maniacal power. Even Neely Kate. Why in the hell would she want to have any sort of relationship with *me*?"

Rose moved next to me. "You're just as much a victim in this."

I violently shook my head. "*Don't.* Don't go there. You kept warning me that he would hurt you, and I refused to listen. I put you in danger."

"Joe." She rested her hand on my arm. "It's done. Clean slate." She grabbed my arm and turned me to face her. "There's a great man inside of you, Joe. A man you've always been destined to be, but your father held you back. Hilary held you back. You're free. *You can do this.*" Then she threw her arms around my neck and pulled me into a hug.

Something in me stirred. Part of me still loved her. I was sure I'd always love her, but Mason was right. She needed to be free for a while, to see who she was meant to be without having to answer to anyone.

"I'll always be sorry I lost you," I whispered in her ear.

She froze, but then leaned back and gave me another sad smile. "You haven't lost me, Joe. Our relationship's changed is all. We're friends. And I know that in time you'll find a woman who will be good for you. I'm just not her."

While part of me knew that, the rest of me still mourned the loss of her. "I know."

"I'm still here for you. Whatever you need. Whenever you need it. But *please*, I'm begging you, reach out to Neely Kate. She's devastated, Joe."

A new wave of guilt washed through me, but I still wasn't ready to face her.

Rose hesitated and gave me a guilty look. "If you'd like, I can tell you with certainty that everything will be okay."

"What do you mean?"

"I can have a vision. I can look for when you're happy. I can tell you what I see." When I didn't answer, she said, "I can do this, Joe. I can look for specific things now. It's how I saved Mason."

I stared at her in disbelief as the truth hit me. "That's why you became the Lady in Black. You questioned criminals."

She stiffened. "I did what I had to do to protect him."

"Who did you talk to?"

Her guard went up. "Is this an official police investigation?"

I ran my hand through my hair. "God, no, Rose. How can you ask me that? I'm asking as your friend."

"You weren't my friend when you arrested me for a murder you knew full well I didn't commit."

I took several steps away, my frustration growing. We'd had this argument more times than I could count, and it never ended well. "Rose, I'm currently on leave from the sheriff's department, and I suspect half the people you questioned are now dead. You've given up your alter ego, so what would it serve legally?" I paused. "You just caught me off guard. I still think of you as the woman who needed protecting. Thinking of you alone with those criminals scares the shit out of me."

She bit her lower lip, then said, "I wasn't alone. I had protection."

"You had a gun?"

"No." She shook her head. "Well, a gun later, but I was talking about a person."

My stomach fell. "Skeeter Malcolm." I turned to look at her. "How'd you get involved with him?"

"Off the record?"

"I told you—"

"I need your word that you'll never take what I tell you and use it against him."

My mouth dropped open. "You're protecting him."

Her chin lifted in defiance. "He protected *me*."

"You like him?" It was more of a statement.

Her back stiffened. "We're friends."

"You're friends with a criminal? A crime lord. *A murderer.*"

"That's not the man I know, Joe."

"Yet that's the man he is, Rose!"

"No. He's more than that."

I studied her closely. Why was she protecting him? Had Mason left because she was sleeping with Malcolm?

But I knew her. She would never cheat, and there was no denying she'd loved Mason. I was pretty sure she still did, even months later. Watching her now, she had the same fierce stance she took when she was defending Neely Kate. Malcolm really was her friend, although I wasn't so sure why that surprised me. Look at Bruce Wayne. And Jonah Pruitt. She picked the most unlikely people as friends.

People like me.

"I promise," I said. "We're having this conversation as friends. I won't use anything against him."

But she still hesitated. "I was the one to go to him. I made the rules. He risked his life to protect me."

I slowly shook my head. "There's no way Malcolm would risk his life for you. Especially if you needed him to help the assistant DA. What did you give him?" While I waited for her to answer, I started connecting the dots. "You questioned criminals. You gave him information."

"There were people out to kill him too," she said with no sign of guilt. "I was protecting them both."

I was pretty sure she had given him other information as well, but I wasn't about to call her on it.

I didn't feel like fighting with her. "Are you still working with him?"

"You mean am I still questioning people for him?" She shook her head. "I hung up my hat and veil after I confronted your father."

But she was still friends with him. I could see it in her eyes. As much as I wanted to warn her to stay away from him, I'd learned that ordering Rose around was not the way to get things accomplished.

"No lectures?" she asked with a hint of attitude.

"No. I'd tell you to be careful, but I already know you are."

She looked surprised for a second, but then she grinned. "There might be hope for you yet, Joe Simmons."

I was beginning to think she was right.

Chapter Six

Rose

Joe seemed better when I left him, yet I still drove away with a heavy heart. I'd tried one more time to convince him to talk to Neely Kate, but he'd deflected the suggestion, saying he needed to get back to working on the house. When I asked for a tour, he told me I'd given him too much thinking to do but promised to give me one later.

Rain began to fall as I headed back into town, and Muffy jumped onto my lap when a loud crack of thunder ripped through the air.

"That was close, huh, Muff?" I covered her back with my hand to help control her shaking. I couldn't help thinking I should have left her with Joe for the afternoon. He seemed so lonely, and they loved each other.

A flash of lightning touched down close to the neighborhood where Bruce Wayne and the crew were working, and less than half a minute later my phone rang. I checked my caller ID before I answered, slightly worried when I saw Bruce Wayne's name. Bruce Wayne rarely called. He was more of a texting guy.

Pulling over to the side of the road, I turned on my hazard lights. The rain was coming down in sheets, making it too dangerous to take the call while driving.

"Is everything okay?" I asked. "Did you get caught in the storm?"

"We got our tools packed up before it hit. I sent the crew home for the day. We'll start again tomorrow if it's not too muddy. But that's not why I'm calling."

I started to panic. "Are you okay? Anna?"

"Rose," he said in a gentle voice. "We're fine."

"Okay."

"This is going to sound weird, but I'm calling about our client's neighbor."

"Heidi Joy?"

"She the one with all the kids? The one you were talking to earlier?"

"Yeah," I said. Another bolt of lightning flashed through the sky, and I snuggled my shaking dog closer. "She was my next-door neighbor when I lived in Momma's house. What about her?"

"Her dog ran off."

"Oh no." My heart plummeted.

"I'm only calling because she has some crazy idea that you might know how to find her dog. Now, why would she think that?"

I groaned. "I had a vision. I saw Hugo running away and her boys chasing him. I blurted out that he was going to run away because of the storm, but I have no idea where he got off to."

"With all them kids, she can't leave, and she's worried. She wants you to give her a call."

"I'll call, but the last time I tried to get ahold of her, it said the number was out of service."

"She says she changed phones and lost all her numbers. But I'll text it to you. I didn't want to give yours out without asking you first."

"Thanks." I wasn't sure what I could do, but calling her back seemed like the right thing to do. The rain had begun to let up some, but my truck was old enough that it didn't have a Bluetooth hookup, so I decided to wait until I got back to the office to make the call.

Once I was parked on the town square, I scooped up Muffy and ran. The door to the office opened as I reached it. Neely Kate stood to the side.

"What took you so long? I was worried," she said.

"I got delayed." I wanted to tell her about Joe, but now didn't seem like the best time. "You'll never guess who I saw."

"Who?" she asked as she shut the door behind us.

"Heidi Joy. My old neighbor. She and her family live next door to the house Bruce Wayne and his crew are working on."

"Wow. Small world."

"I had a vision while I was there." I told her what I'd seen and how I'd played it off. This next part would be tricky since I wasn't ready to tell her about Joe. "After I left, the storm hit and Bruce Wayne called with a message from Heidi Joy. Her dog Hugo ran off, and she's desperate to find him. She asked me to call her, which I still need to do."

"Oh, dear," Neely Kate said, glancing down at Muffy.

I was sure we were thinking the same thing. What would we do if we lost my little dog?

"I wish I could do more to help," I said. "I have no idea where he went."

"Why don't you put her on speaker phone? Maybe we can figure something out."

I rolled my office chair across the wooden floor to Neely Kate's desk, then pulled my phone out of my pocket. After I dialed Heidi Joy's number, I set the phone on the desk.

"Rose?" Heidi Joy asked. "Is that you?"

I cast a glance to Neely Kate, then looked back at the phone. "It's me, but I have Neely Kate on the phone too. Bruce Wayne told me about Hugo."

"You warned us he was gonna run off, and we tried to keep him in, but Tommy was watching the landscaping crew load up their truck. He opened the front storm door without giving it a second thought, and Hugo ran out."

"I'm so sorry," I said. "I take it he hasn't come back yet?"

"No." She sniffled, and the crying I heard in the background grew louder. "I'm stuck here with all the kids. I don't know how you knew Hugo was gonna run off, but I'm begging you, Rose. If you have any idea where he might have gone, please tell me."

"I don't, Heidi Joy," I said, my heart breaking for her and the boys. "It was only a guess."

"Which way did he run?" Neely Kate asked as she leaned closer to the phone.

"He ran down the street," Heidi Joy said. "Toward the McManus farm."

I shot Neely Kate a questioning glance, but she ignored me. "Has he run away before?"

"A few times."

"And where did you find him before?"

"Once at the farm. The other two times we found him in our neighborhood."

"We have to go see a client out your way," Neely Kate said. "We'll look for him while we're out."

My eyebrows shot up. I mouthed, *What are you doing?* But Neely Kate kept her attention on the phone.

"Oh, would you?" Heidi Joy asked, her voice breaking. "My boys are devastated."

Neely Kate reached to get her purse from her open bottom desk drawer. "We're just about to head out. If you hear anything, give Rose a call."

"Thank you so much!"

Neely Kate ended the call, then handed me the phone.

I stood and rolled my chair back to my desk. "What are you doing, Neely Kate? We weren't headed out that way."

"We need the experience," she said as she turned her computer off. "We can add this to our résumé."

"What résumé?"

"Our detective work résumé."

"Neely Kate. We are *not* detectives."

"Bull hockey. We've solved all kinds of dangerous and non-dangerous mysteries. And we've even gotten paid for solving a crime."

"For finding a garden gnome, Neely Kate!"

"We made $500!"

I rolled my eyes. "I'll help look for Hugo because I'm worried about him, not because I'm interested in adding anything to our résumé."

She gave me a smug look. "Whatever you want to call it, it serves the same purpose."

The storm had let up, so I grabbed Muffy's leash and headed to the front door, Muffy prancing after me. "Let's go find your new friend."

We all climbed into my truck and rolled down the windows, letting fresh air fill the cab.

"What neighborhood was Bruce Wayne's job at?" Neely Kate asked as I drove away from the square. "She mentioned the McManus farm. Was it the one in Briar Patch Acres?"

"Yup. We should probably drive up and down the streets and look for him first."

"Good idea," she said. "What's he look like?"

"He's bigger than Muffy. I would guess about fifteen pounds. He's furry—mostly white, with some black spots. Little ears that flop over. He's cute."

"The kind of dog people might steal."

I shot her an anxious look. "They got him from an animal shelter."

She shrugged, but she looked about as worried as I felt. "The sooner we find him, the better."

When we reached the neighborhood, we drove slowly down the streets, calling out Hugo's name. After we made it through twice, I called Heidi Joy.

"Have you found him?" she asked as soon as she answered.

"No," I said, putting the phone on speaker so Neely Kate could join the conversation. "I was hoping you'd heard something."

"No."

"Hey," Neely Kate said. "Does he have a chip?"

"Yes. He was neutered and chipped when we adopted him."

"Maybe it has GPS tracking," Neely Kate suggested.

"No," Heidi Joy said, sounding forlorn. "It only scans at the vet if he's found."

"Okay," I said. "We're going to keep looking. I'll let you know if we have any news."

"I'll do the same."

Muffy released a soft whine when we ended the call.

"It's okay, girl. We'll find him," I said.

The farm backed up to the edge of the road, so we parked the truck and I attached Muffy's leash. We walked the fence, looking for any signs.

"There," Neely Kate said, pointing to some paw prints in the mud. "Do you think that could be from Hugo?"

"Yeah," I said, leaning forward. "It definitely could." But I pushed out a sigh when I realized the prints went under the wooden fence and continued into a soybean field.

Neely Kate cupped her hands around her mouth and shouted, "Hugo!"

We waited for several seconds before I called out his name too.

"Now what?" Neely Kate asked.

I looked her over and shook my head, handing her my car keys. "I'll walk through the field and look for him. You drive the truck over to the McManus farmhouse and wait for me." Before she could object, I waved to her shoes. "You can't go traipsing through the fields in those. They'll get ruined."

She shuffled in her pink, glitter-covered flats. "I didn't plan on working out in the field today, and my work boots are back at the office."

"It's okay," I said with a smile. "I could use a walk to clear my head."

Her eyes narrowed. "Why do you need to clear your head?"

Crappy doodles. I didn't want to have this conversation now. "Sometimes a girl just needs a moment to think." I unhooked Muffy's leash and started to climb over the wooden fence. "Call me if you find him."

I planned to spend most of this walk trying to figure out how to tell Neely Kate I'd seen her brother.

Chapter Seven
Neely Kate

Rose was hiding something.

I knew her well enough to know the difference between when she was sad and needed space and when she was up to something. And this was the latter.

It wasn't hard to figure out what she was hiding. She'd been gone for over an hour and a half this afternoon, and her timeline didn't add up.

She'd gone to see Joe.

It didn't take a genius to see she was keeping it a big secret, but it wasn't hard to figure out. Joe must have told her he didn't want to have anything to do with me.

The realization set me reeling, but it only took a second for the lightheadedness to go away. The hurt, I was used to. This wasn't the first time someone in my family had found me lacking.

By the time I'd walked back to the truck and driven toward the road, Rose had climbed the fence and was already twenty feet into the field, with no sign of Muffy.

But that wasn't unusual. Rose let Muffy walk off-leash in the fields by her farm all the time.

I had to pay close attention when I got to the main road. I knew the general location of the entrance to the farm, but it wasn't marked. I took a wrong turn and had to backtrack, but Rose still wasn't there when I pulled up in front of the McManus house and barn.

There weren't any cars parked out front, but I got out of the truck and walked up to the front door and knocked. I didn't know much about the McManuses, beyond that they were a middle-aged couple with grown kids, but I figured it was better to let them know Rose was walking across their field before someone walked out with a shotgun. Several knocks later, no one had come to the door.

They weren't home.

I sat on the steps to the front porch while I waited. Trying to think about anything besides the last few months. Ronnie had taken off at the beginning of February, and I hadn't heard a word from him since. I'd gone to Carter Hale, the attorney who'd represented Rose when she was charged with murder, and asked him to file for divorce. I knew Carter would have to serve him with papers, and I'd hoped his server would flush him out. But three months later, there was still neither hide nor hair of him.

While Rose was in Houston, I'd gone to talk to Skeeter Malcolm. It was something I'd considered doing before, but her absence meant I wouldn't have to come up with an excuse. I'd stopped by the pool hall on my way back to the office after a landscaping consult. The place was deserted, but I was still surprised to see Skeeter and Jed playing pool.

"Neither of you boys have real jobs?" I'd asked with a lot of sass as I walked toward them. "You just hang out at the pool hall on any ol' Tuesday afternoon?"

Jed eyed me with his typical stoicism, but Skeeter looked worried. "Is Rose okay?"

That stopped me in my tracks. While it wasn't a secret that Rose had gone to Texas to donate her bone marrow, it wasn't exactly common knowledge either. And while Skeeter liked to keep tabs on all things in Fenton County, this wasn't idle curiosity. It was genuine concern.

Rose had been in contact with Skeeter Malcolm. Why hadn't she told me?

But that was a question for another time. I shook off my surprise and said, "Rose is fine. I'm here for another purpose."

His shit-eating grin didn't quite cover up the look of relief. "You here to give me trouble, Neely Kate?"

I knew Skeeter was waiting for an answer, but I couldn't stop thinking about how concerned he was for Rose. While Rose and I had each other, I wanted someone else to care about me the way Skeeter cared for her. I had thought Ronnie was that person, but I'd driven him away. Maybe I deserved to be alone.

I was about to give Skeeter some sassy retort, but to my horror, my chin trembled and tears filled my eyes.

Jed's expression changed on a dime. Without saying a word, he moved toward me, wrapped an arm around my back, and led me to the office down the hall. After he got me settled into a chair in front of Skeeter's desk, Skeeter appeared in the doorway with a bottle of water. He shut the door behind him and then sat in the chair next to me rather than the one behind the desk. Jed stayed right where he was, standing by my side.

"Are you in some kind of trouble?" Skeeter asked.

I started laughing even as tears flowed down my cheeks. "I'm always in some kind of trouble. You should know that by now." I grabbed the water bottle out of his hand and took a sip.

Skeeter looked up at Jed, then back to me. "Is this about your husband?"

I nodded, but I couldn't look him in the eye. "I need answers, Skeeter. I need to find him. Will you help me?"

He was silent for a moment before he said, "I don't know where he is, Neely Kate. We've already looked."

My head jerked up. "You what?"

He held my gaze. "Jed and Merv have both been following leads, but they haven't found anything."

Fear shot through me like an arrow. "Oh, my God. Are you after him because he sided with Gentry?"

Skeeter sat back with a look of disgust. "We're lookin' for him for *you*. Because you need to find him. You didn't ask us to, but we wanted to help you."

His statement could have knocked me over with a feather. I knew Skeeter cared about Rose, but why would he give two figs about me?

I was about to ask him when a knock landed on the door.

A dark shadow crossed over his face as he called out, "*What?*"

The door opened and the bartender appeared in the doorframe. He looked almost as scared as he had that time Skeeter flew off the handle when he discovered Rose and me questioning Dirk Picklebie. "Mr. Malcolm, there's someone from the sheriff's department asking for you."

Skeeter grimaced and rose from his chair.

I looked up at him with alarm. "Are *you* in trouble?"

A smirk lit up his eyes. "Just like you, NK, I'm always in some kind of trouble. But in this instance, they're probably here about the whole Simmons mess."

"Joe's dad?"

"They keep coming by to see if I've remembered anything else. And every time they show up, I tell them nothing's changed." He looked over my head at Jed. "You got this?"

Jed nodded. "Yeah."

Skeeter gave him a long look, then walked out of the office and shut the door behind him.

We were silent for several seconds before Jed sat in the seat Skeeter had vacated. He rested his forearms on the chair arms. "Neely Kate, I hate to ask, but have you considered the possibility that Ronnie might be dead?"

I'd considered it every day since Ronnie had stopped returning my calls. Sure, he'd turned out to be a different man from the one I'd married, but I knew his heart. That man had loved me. He'd loved the babies we'd lost. I understood why he'd left me. But I couldn't see him doing it without a word. "Yes."

"Yet you filed for divorce anyway?"

I took another drink of water. "I was trying to draw him out of hiding. It didn't work."

"I don't think he's going to turn up, Neely Kate. Can you deal with that?"

"I guess I'll have to, won't I?"

He shifted in his chair and then looked into my eyes. "You know that I protect Rose when she needs it, but I'm here for you too. If you ever need anything at all, I want you to call me."

What was he telling me? "Because of Skeeter and Rose?"

"No," he said, speaking so quietly I could barely hear him. "Because of you."

Suddenly the room seemed to grow five times smaller, and I found it difficult to catch my breath. "I need to go," I said as I jumped to my feet. "Would you and Skeeter please keep my visit to yourselves?"

Jed stood and moved between me and the door, blocking my path of escape. "Rose doesn't know you're here? Don't you think she'd understand?"

"She'd understand all too well. I'm trying to convince her I'm fine while she tries to convince me she's fine." My frustration grew. "I'm tired of feeling this way, Jed. I'm tired of feeling like crap."

"I know."

"You want to know the crazy part?" I asked, feeling dangerously close to losing it. "I wasn't even in love with him. I loved him. I cared about him. But I wasn't in love with him."

He didn't answer, just searched my face and waited for me to continue.

My anxiety got the better of me and I asked, "You ever been in love, Jed?"

He hesitated, then asked, "How are things between you and Joe?"

"Oh, my stars and garters!" I shouted. "You are so frustrating!"

"I'm only trying to help, Neely Kate."

And that was the problem. It made me nervous that he *cared* to try, and I wasn't sure what to make of it. People didn't make me nervous. Situations, yes, but never people. Jed had me tied up in knots. "I have to go."

"You said that already."

Putting my hand on my hip, I gave him my haughtiest attitude. "You're blocking my path."

A slow grin cracked his lips. "Then why don't you ask me to move?"

"Get the hell out of my way, Jed, or I'll turn you into a eunuch with my boot."

He laughed and I tried to think of any time I'd seen him belly laugh like that. Something warm and tingly danced in my stomach. Jed was a handsome man, but when he laughed, it was hard to look away.

Oh, my stars and garters. Do not fall for Jed.

He stepped to the side and reached for the doorknob, but his hand lingered there. His face turned serious again. "I'm here for you too, Neely Kate. Don't forget it."

I shoved his hand out of the way and opened the door. He followed me out of the office as I entered the pool hall. Two sheriff's deputies were talking to Skeeter, but he looked about as bored and testy as a caged lion at the zoo.

A dog's bark coming from the fields jarred me back to the present. Rose was heading toward the house, but before she could reach me, something white and black ran out of the soybean plants and headed straight for the barn.

"We didn't find him," Rose shouted as she got closer.

"I think I just did." I hopped to my feet and ran toward the barn. "He went in here."

"Really?" she asked, perking up.

I opened the barn door and stepped right into the darkness, walking around an old tractor. "Come here, Hugo. It's okay."

I saw him run out from under the tractor into the back corner. Rose and Muffy had reached the doorway, and Muffy, who was normally as sweet as could be, released a low growl.

"Muffy," I said as I moved toward the animal huddled in the corner. "Be nice to Hugo." I grabbed Hugo and hefted him into my arms, surprised at his weight. I didn't have much experience with dogs, but Muffy didn't feel this firm and round. "Hugo needs to go on a diet."

"Uh, Neely Kate . . ." Rose said anxiously. "What are you doing?"

"Getting Hugo."

"Hugo's *a dog*."

"Duh. I know."

"Then why in tarnation are you holding a baby pig?"

"What?" I stepped into the light and saw that I was indeed holding a baby pig. I screamed and half-tossed it to the ground. It landed on its feet and took off squealing. "Oh, my stars and garters! I was holding a pig!" I took off running to the truck to get my hand sanitizer out of my purse while Rose's laughter followed behind me.

"How did you think *that* was Hugo?"

I jerked the truck door open and started to rummage around in my purse. "I saw something white and black duck in the crack in the barn door, and it looked about the right size! We need to get out of here."

"We can't leave it running loose," she said. "We have to catch it."

I put some of the sanitizer on my hands. Then another squeeze for good measure. "I'm not touching that pig again!" I shouted even though I knew she was right.

"Neely Kate!"

I glanced back over my shoulder and saw the pig crawl under a wooden fence to an empty horse enclosure. "I can't go in there with my shoes."

Rose released a groan as she went around to the driver's side of the truck. She emerged with an open bag of chips. "I figure if Muffy likes these things, the baby pig will too."

"Just don't fall down in there," I said as I followed her to the fence. "It might eat you."

She glanced over her shoulder at me, giving me a look that said I'd lost my mind.

"I'm serious," I said. "If we ever need to dispose of a body, I'm taking it out to the Vernon pig farm."

"Remind me to never tick you off." She stuck her hand in the bag and pulled out several chips. Muffy pranced around at her feet, begging for a treat. "You hold onto this," Rose said as she handed me the bag. "And keep Muffy out of the pen."

I squatted and wrapped an arm around the dog. The chip bag in my free hand had Muffy's undivided attention. "I think you should rethink this. It's not like we let it out. This isn't worth getting eaten over."

"That piglet's not going to eat me," she groaned as she climbed over the fence. "But it's a darn good thing I wore my work jeans today."

And it was a darn good thing I *hadn't*, but I figured that was something better kept to myself.

Rose clomped across the enclosure in her already muddy boots. When she got close, she hunkered down and tossed a potato chip to the cowering pig. It started snorting, then gobbled up the chip and moved closer to Rose, its nose jiggling as it smelled its way toward her. Rose tossed several more chips onto the ground, and when the piglet stooped down to eat them, she scooped it up into her arms, holding it tight against her stomach.

"Now what do we do with it?" I asked as she left the enclosure, her arms wrapped around the piglet.

"Can you see where they keep it?"

I glanced around and saw a pen on the other side of the barn, but a toppled tree had smashed part of the wire enclosure.

"Well, crap," I muttered. "Now what do we do?"

"What if there were more pigs?" Rose asked.

"I'll find out." Groaning, I pulled my phone out of my pocket and called my cousin. "Witt? What do you know about the McManus farm?"

"Why? What kind of trouble have you gotten into now?"

"Long story short, we found a baby pig."

"What? On their farm?"

"Of course on their farm. How else would I know it was their pig? It's not like he has a collar with a name tag." I glanced over at Rose and whispered, "It doesn't have a collar, does it?"

She grinned and shook her head.

Witt groaned. "I'm not sure I want to know why you're asking about the McManus prize pig, but I suggest you put it back where you found it. George wants to enter it into the county fair when it's full grown."

"We can't put it back where we got it. He was running loose in the fields. It looks like his pen got knocked out in the storm."

"I take it they're not home?"

"I wouldn't be callin' you if they were."

"Take it to the new vet. Dr. Romano," Witt said. "He took over for Dr. Ritchie. I hear he takes rescue animals, so if you can't pen him up, you can take him there."

"You expect us to take this pig to the vet's?"

"Unless you've got a better idea."

I was about to tell him what he could do with his idea, but he hung up.

Rose's eyes were wide. "Please tell me we're not taking this pig in the truck."

I grinned. "I guess we could tie a rope around his neck and tie him to the fence post."

"Crappy doodles," she groaned. "It's not going into the cab. What if it poops?"

"We can't leave it in the back by itself," I countered. "Someone's got to ride with it." I looked down at my white capri pants and sparkly shoes before glancing back up at her with an ornery grin.

Rose muttered under her breath as she started walking toward the truck. I lowered the tailgate, and she put the pig on the bed and climbed in with it. As I shut the tailgate, she gave me a look that told me I'd be paying for this for some time to come. I made a mental note to buy more sparkly shoes.

Muffy climbed into the cab with me, then jumped into the rear seat and watched Rose and the pig in the back.

Lucky for us, the vet's office was on this side of town, just outside the city limits. The parking lot was nearly empty when we pulled in. I hopped out and went inside, leaving Rose in the back with the pig and Muffy in the cab.

The receptionist looked up in surprise. She was a middle-aged woman with crazy brunette hair that looked like she'd stuck her finger in a light socket. "Are you here to pick up a dog from the groomer?"

"No. Actually I'm here to drop off a pig."

"*Excuse me?*"

"I hear Dr. Romano takes rescue animals."

She looked taken aback. "Sure. Dogs and cats, but a *pig?*"

A man who looked like he was in his late twenties appeared in the hallway. "Did you say *a pig?*"

He was a fine-looking man—light brown hair, blue eyes, and he filled out the shoulders of his white lab coat quite nicely. This was the first time I'd seen him for myself, but I'd already heard a thing or two about him around town. Now that Mason had left and the mayor had gone back to his wife, the title of Most Eligible Bachelor in Fenton County had briefly fallen to Bubba Ramsey, which meant times had *truly* gotten desperate. Dr. Levi Romano, on the other hand, fit the vacated position all too well. Too bad for Bubba.

"It's the McManuses' pig," I said, trying not to be so obvious about checking him out. "My cousin says they're raising it for the county fair. We couldn't just leave it running around, but we weren't sure what to do with it."

He took several steps toward me, drying off his hands with a paper towel. "I take it the McManuses aren't home."

"No."

"Do you have it with you?" he asked, searching the small waiting area, although I had no idea where he thought I might be hiding a pig, baby or not. The room was full of folding chairs, a beat-up end table, and ten-year-old magazines with headlines like "Understanding Your Schnauzer" and "101 Ways to Make Your Cat Love You."

"Out in the truck."

"Mary," he said, sounding amused. "I'll be right back."

Mary muttered something about Noah's Ark, but the vet ignored her.

"I'm Dr. Romano, by the way," he said as he followed me out the door. Which meant he had a full view of my backside. I'd sat on the steps at the McManus house. What if I had a giant stain in the middle of one of my butt cheeks?

Why hadn't I thought to check?

"So I've heard," I said as I kept moving around the back of the truck.

Poor Rose looked like she was at her wits' end. The piglet was running circles around her, squealing like a . . . well, like a pig, while Muffy barked her protest in the back window.

"So this is the pig," Dr. Romano said with a grin, resting his hands on the tailgate.

"I don't know about you, Rose," I said dryly. "But I'm already feeling confident about Dr. Romano's veterinarian abilities and observational skills."

He laughed and lowered the tailgate. "Since it's a special pig, does it have a name?"

I started to offer a witty retort, but Rose answered first. "Not that we know of. We were tracking a lost dog to the McManus farm, and Neely Kate rescued this little guy out of the barn after she saw it go inside."

He took in Rose's muddy boots and jeans, and I could see the question in his eyes.

I gave him a half-shrug. "Rose then caught him from a mud pit."

He laughed. "Sounds like you both are heroes." He held out his hands as if he was about to catch the pig, but it ran behind Rose and started rutting at her backside.

"Oh, my word," she gasped, scooting to the edge of the tailgate.

Muffy's barking changed into the warning bark she reserved for threats.

"Muffy, calm down," Rose said as she jumped out and onto the ground.

Dr. Romano leaned forward, grabbed hold of the pig's middle, and slid it toward him, the pig squealing in protest all the while.

"What will you do with him?" Rose asked.

"I'll put it in a large pen in the back."

Once he had a firm grip on the pig, Rose hurried over to the door and held it open. Then we both followed him inside and down the hall, past the disapproving receptionist. He pushed through a door, then led the way into a room lined with mostly empty cages. He gestured with his elbow to a cage at the bottom. "Can one of you get that?"

I got the pen open, and he shoved the screaming pig inside, then shut the door behind it.

"Whew," he said. "Thanks for the assist."

"So what happens to him now?" Rose asked.

"I'll have Mary call the McManus farm and let them know they can pick up their pig." He gave me a beaming grin. "Did you happen to find your lost dog?"

"He's not ours," I said. "It's Rose's old neighbor's—never mind. Let's just say he belongs to a friend."

"Was he chipped?"

"Yeah," Rose said. "But he's really cute, so we're worried someone might have picked him up. The owners really love him. Their kids are devastated."

"Any idea where he might have gone?"

"No," Rose said with a frown. "I tracked him into the McManus fields, but that's where I lost track of his paw prints."

"Have you checked the animal shelter?" Dr. Romano asked.

Rose grimaced. "No."

"Mary can give you the number."

"Thanks," she said, looking worried.

Dr. Romano followed us to the receptionist's desk. "If you tell me a bit about the dog, I'll keep an eye out for him."

"That would be great," Rose said. "He's about as tall as the baby pig, and he's white with black spots."

Dr. Romano smirked. "Like the pig."

"Hey!" I said, putting my hands on my hips. "In my defense, I've never seen Hugo before and the barn was dark."

"Hugo?" Dr. Romano asked. "The family he belongs to wouldn't happen to have a bunch of kids, mostly boys?"

Rose laughed. "That's the one."

"Yes, I know them. I'll keep my eye out," he said. "If you ladies will leave your number, I'll let you know if Hugo shows up here."

"That would be great," Rose said, grabbing a piece of paper that Mary was already handing her. "Thank you."

"No problem at all."

Muffy was barking her outrage over being left, but she quieted down as soon as we were back in the cab of the truck.

"Where do we look now?" Rose asked as she turned on the engine, then rubbed Muffy's head to reassure her.

"You're really not going to address the fact that Dr. Romano, the town's newest, most eligible bachelor, just hit on you?"

Rose gasped and turned to me with a mixture of shock and irritation. "What are you talking about?"

"You really didn't realize he was hitting on you?"

"No. I talked to the veterinarian about the McManus pig and Hugo. You talked to him more than I did. If he was hitting on anyone, it was you."

"He asked for your number, Rose."

"He asked for *our* number so he could tell us if Hugo shows up. Our number. Both of us. And he was just being helpful."

"He was looking right at you. Smiling. He wanted *your* number."

She scowled and flipped down the visor to look at her face in the mirror. "Oh, my word. What are you

86

talking about? I look like I was caught out in that storm myself."

She was right. From her muddy pants and boots to her ragged ponytail and reddened cheeks, she looked like she'd had a long day chasing around dogs and pigs. But she was still pretty.

"You're the one looking cute today. If he was interested in either of us, it had to be you," she said, flipping the visor back up. Then she turned in her seat and looked me right in the eye. "Are you thinking about dating? Does his being interested in you make you nervous?"

Jed's face instantly popped into my head. "Of course I'm not interested in dating. I'm not even divorced."

"You may not be divorced for a long time if Carter's PI can't find Ronnie. He still hasn't turned up."

I considered telling her about my visit to Skeeter weeks ago, but I worried I'd let on about my complicated feelings for Jed. Besides, I still didn't want her to know how badly I needed closure. I was tired of looking weak and pathetic. I needed to suck it up and move on.

But Rose continued. "He clearly abandoned you, Neely Kate. If you feel like you're ready to date again, then you should."

"What about you?" I asked. "You weren't even married. *You* could date if you wanted to."

She was quiet for a moment, then said softly, "I still love Mason."

I put my hand over hers and patted it. "I know."

She turned to look at me. "But sometimes I wonder if I should date anyway. Maybe it wouldn't hurt so much if I dated someone else. But I worry about jumping into a new relationship too soon, like I did with Mason."

"Do you know what I think?" I asked.

She searched my face, waiting.

"I think you'll know when the time's right. I think we both will. Until then, we'll just live in your house with Muffy, and all three of us can become spinsters together."

Rose laughed and Muffy barked her approval.

And I couldn't help thinking that might not be so bad.

So why did I feel a huge hole in my heart?

Part Three

Chapter Eight

Rose

Neely Kate called the animal shelter as I drove toward town, but Hugo hadn't shown up.

"You told Dr. Romano that his paw prints disappeared in the field," Neely Kate said. "Did you see where they might have headed?"

"No," I said. "The prints were in mud, but I lost them in a section that was covered with leaves. If I had to guess, I think he might have been headed toward the woods." I cast a glance toward her. "But they might not have even been Hugo's paw prints. Maybe we should give up. For all we know, he'll come home on his own."

"But it's a case!" Neely Kate protested. "And I know it's a small one, but the more solved cases we have under our belts, the better for our résumé." When I hesitated, she added, "Heidi Joy would have called us if he'd turned up, and just think about those disappointed boys. Do you really want to quit now?"

I groaned. "No, but it feels like we're looking for a needle in a haystack."

"Let's go check out the woods. If we don't find him there, we'll figure out our next steps."

Neely Kate studied the GPS on her phone, giving me directions to a section of trees on the east side of the farm that was close to a county road. When we reached the spot she'd found, I parked the truck and glanced down at Neely Kate's feet.

"I guess you'll have to stay by the truck."

She gave me an apologetic look. "I'll make sure Hugo doesn't get away if he comes out."

I laughed. "I'm not sure there's enough stain remover in all of Arkansas to get muddy dog stains out of those pants."

"Hey," Neely Kate said indignantly. "I need to do my part."

I pulled her in for a hug. "You do your part and more. I'm not sure how I would have survived these last few months without you."

She leaned back and pushed me away. "Go find Hugo. I'm hungry."

I'd been hungry before our visit to the vet, but our conversation about dating had stolen my appetite. I hadn't thought about dating. Part of me had hoped Mason would move back to Henryetta, although I knew that wasn't going to happen. Maeve had hinted that he loved his new job in the state attorney's office.

He was moving on, and I needed to do the same.

I forced a smile. "Just a warning—skunks are black and white too, but Hugo's more white and black. Kind of like that pig."

She stuck out her tongue. "Very funny. Just for that, if you get lost in the woods, I'm not ruining my sparkly new shoes to come find you."

That was a lie, and we both knew it.

I slipped into the woods and headed toward the farm, calling out Hugo's name every few steps. After I'd gone about twenty feet, I heard whimpering. I followed the sound and was surprised to see a white and black furball, covered in mud, stuck in something close to a tree.

"Hugo?" I called out as I moved closer.

The dog lifted his head and tried to run toward me—but he didn't get very far. As I got closer, I realized he was snagged in some sort of netting that was stuck to the bark on a tree.

"Hey, buddy," I said, rubbing his head to help settle him down. He was wet and shaking, either from fear or from being wet. Probably both. "Got stuck, huh?"

I started feeling his feet to figure out *how* he'd gotten stuck. The net had wrapped around his left front paw. At first I tried to untangle him, but then I simply jerked the net from the tree. I scooped him up and held him to my side as rain began to fall again.

When I emerged from the woods, Neely Kate was standing next to the truck, holding an umbrella over her head. Her eyes widened when she saw me.

"You found him?"

"Yeah, but he's got something wrapped around his leg. He was caught on a tree. I think there's a pocket knife in the glove compartment. Can you get it?"

"Yeah," she said, already rounding the front of the truck. She was back with the blade within seconds.

I held Hugo close as she cut the netting from his leg.

"Is his leg okay?" I asked. "Do we need to take him back to the vet?"

Neely Kate laughed. "So you decided to give Dr. Romano a shot?"

"No!" I said, getting irritated, although I had no idea why. "I'm worried about Hugo."

"Well, I think he's fine, but we can always run back to the vet's office if you want a second opinion."

I shot her an exasperated look. "If his leg looks fine, then we should take him home. Unless *you* want to take him in." I lifted my eyebrows to get my point across.

But Neely Kate seemed unfazed. She just chuckled and said, "Then let's get this little guy home."

There was no denying that Hugo was a muddy mess, and so was I, but I didn't feel like riding in the back again, and I wasn't about to let Hugo loose in the cab of my truck. We decided that I'd sit on the passenger seat and hold Hugo while Neely Kate drove; then we'd clean off the vinyl seat when we got home. I wondered how Muffy would take this arrangement, but she whimpered as she sniffed Hugo's head and even licked his face a few times.

"Looks like one of us is ready to start dating," Neely Kate laughed. "One less spinster at the Gardner farm."

Heidi Joy's front door opened as soon as we pulled up to the curb, and four little boys spilled out, nearly tripping each other. Hugo caught sight of them as soon as the door opened, and he started squirming and whining until I opened the truck door. I hadn't planned to put him down—I didn't want him running off again—but he wiggled out of my hold and landed on his feet. He took off running, but this time he headed straight for the boys.

They threw their arms around him, all four shouting Hugo's name and telling him how much they'd missed him.

Heidi Joy made her way outside, with her youngest boy clinging to her legs and her baby on her hip, and looked up at us in amazement. "You found him."

"We did," Neely Kate said, grinning from ear to ear.

"How?" Heidi Joy asked.

"We thought we found his tracks," I said. "So I followed them onto the McManus farm, but then we lost them. After Neely Kate pulled up a map of the area, we checked the woods next to the farm and found the spot where it connects to the farm. Poor little guy was caught in what looked like a fishing net, although I have no idea how a fishing net got out there. I got him loose, and Neely Kate said his leg looked okay, but you might want to check it out after you give him a bath."

"He was stuck?" Heidi Joy asked, wiping a tear from her eye. "You two saved him. I know the woods on the east side of the farm. The Whites own it, and they rarely go out there. We never would have found him."

"Well, he's safe now, and the boys are happy," I said. "We're just happy to have helped."

Heidi Joy wrung her hands, still distraught. "Is there anything I can do to repay you?"

Neely Kate shook her head. "We were happy to do it. If you want, you can tell your friends we're good at solving cases."

I shot Neely Kate a look and shook my head in bemusement. She was bound and determined to make us investigators.

"I will," Heidi Joy said, then looked down at her boys. "Andy Jr., bring Hugo inside and let's get him cleaned up."

"Oh," I said. "You might call Dr. Romano to let him know Hugo's safe."

Her eyebrows shot up in surprise. "You called Dr. Romano? How'd you know he was our vet?"

"Well . . ." Neely Kate drawled. "We happened to stop by about something else and mentioned Hugo was missing. He said he'd keep an eye out."

"I'll call him right away," Heidi Joy said. "Thanks again."

Neely Kate and I got into the truck, and I told her to head home. "I'll just track mud into the office, and it's close to quitting time anyway. I say we go home."

"We can watch a movie," Neely Kate said, "although I think we've seen every chick flick on Netflix rated four stars or higher. Maybe it's time both of us started working on a social life."

"We can start a social life tomorrow," I said. "I have my usual Tuesday night plans."

She shot me her usual questioning look, but she didn't ask; I didn't offer.

After we got to the farmhouse, I took a long shower. When I headed downstairs, the smell of Italian spices hit my nose.

"Are you cooking?" I asked.

"Nothing fancy, just some spaghetti with homemade sauce and some garlic bread I found in the freezer," Neely Kate said, scooping some onto two plates. "And we're eating at the table—with napkins even. After our talk at the vet's, I've decided it's time for both of us to stop moping around."

"We haven't been moping around," I countered, taking the plate she held out. I grabbed a piece of bread from the cookie sheet on the stovetop.

"Okay, maybe we've moved past moping, but there's no denying we're stuck in a rut."

I couldn't argue with her there.

"So . . ." she said, giving me a sly look. "Your standing date. You plan to tell me what you're doin'?"

I rolled my eyes. "I'm pretty sure you've figured out what I'm doin'."

"So why the big secret?"

"He thinks it's better this way. He's trying to protect me."

"And how exactly does he go about protecting you?"

I groaned at the insinuation in her voice. "We're just friends, Neely Kate."

"What do you guys do?"

"You know what we do. We talk."

She was dying to know more, but she let it go.

By the time we finished cleaning up the kitchen, it was later than I'd realized. I was about to grab my purse when Neely Kate's phone rang. She looked at the screen and her face paled.

"Who is that?" I asked, worried.

She shook her head and stuffed her phone into her pocket. "Granny."

"Why did you look so startled, then?"

"I wasn't startled. I was terrified. She wants me to take her to bingo."

"I thought Dolly Parton was taking her to bingo these days."

"She must have had something come up."

"Can't you get out of it?"

"I'll take care of it." Neely Kate's phone dinged with a text, but she left it in her pocket.

"Aren't you going to check your message?"

Her upper lip curled with annoyance. "No. They're just tryin' to guilt me into takin' her." She set the dishrag in the sink. "You better get goin'. You don't want to be late."

96

I gave her a long look, then headed out the front door.

I spent most of my fifteen-minute drive wondering who had really texted her and why she'd lied.

Chapter Nine
Joe

I sat on my front porch drinking my third beer of the day. I knew it wouldn't solve anything, but it helped numb my newest pain.

I was too late.

A car drove down the lane, and I sat up to get a better view, but a wave of disappointment washed over me as the car stopped and Maeve got out.

"You could make an old woman paranoid with that look," she said with a laugh. She was carrying a basket, and I could already smell the food inside it.

"Sorry, Maeve. You know I love seeing you—even if you didn't bring me food."

She grinned as she climbed the steps. "So you're saying you don't want me to bring you food?"

My mouth twitched into a grin. "I wouldn't go *that* far."

She set the basket on the table between our chairs, then disappeared into the house. When she came back, a plate and fork in hand, she sat in the empty chair.

"I would have gotten you a drink, but you already seem to have one."

She thought I drank too much, though she was kind enough not to say so outright. I knew it was true, but this one felt warranted. "It's been a rough day." Then I added, "Rose came by this afternoon."

She paused before she said, "Oh." She turned to face me. "Joe, I respected your request. I didn't tell her."

I shrugged and took a swig of my beer. "She found out from someone in town."

"I see." She pulled a container out of the basket and scooped a heaping serving of some sort of delicious-looking casserole onto the plate, then handed it to me. "And how did your visit go?"

"It's Rose. How do you think it went?" I grinned. "A mixture of sweetness and irritation. She yelled. I got mad." Maeve looked worried, but I shook my head. "No, it's good. She told me things that I needed to hear, even if a few of them hurt."

"So does that mean you're ready to go back to work?"

I scowled.

She handed me the plate full of food. "The house looks like it's coming along."

"It's amazing how much I can get done with so much time on my hands."

"So you're thinking about becoming a carpenter?"

"Would that be so bad?"

"Does it give you purpose?"

"Aren't you supposed to ask if it makes me happy?"

"Happiness is fleeting, Joe. Purpose is what we need." She leaned closer. "Does this fill you with purpose? Or does law enforcement?"

"I don't deserve to wear a badge."

"I think this whole mess with your father has made you more deserving than most."

I leaned my head back and groaned. "Maeve."

"You have something to offer, Joe. You have a humbleness about you that you didn't have before." She took a breath and her eyes hardened slightly. "You may not want to hear this, but Mason's demotion to Fenton County made him a better person. It changed him. Rose changed him just like she changed you. She made him see that everything isn't black and white."

"The law requires black and white, Maeve."

"True, in most cases, but Mason learned to show compassion where it was deserved. The FBI showed you compassion; maybe it's your purpose to pay it forward. Maybe you're supposed to show compassion to someone in trouble. Someone who's gotten caught up in something out of their control."

I wasn't convinced it would be that easy, but I understood what she was saying in theory.

"You're good at what you do, Joe, but only you can decide what gives you the most purpose. I'll support you no matter what you decide. Just don't let fear make your choice for you."

"How'd you get so wise?" I asked, taking a bite of her casserole. "And how'd you find time to make this? I thought you and Anna were keeping the nursery open until six, now that the weather's nicer."

She flashed a smile. "I'm a woman of mystery." She stood. "And with that, I'll be off before I spill any of my secrets."

I laughed, but I had to wonder if Maeve had secrets. She seemed to be such an open book.

"Why are you so good to me?" I asked, my voice breaking.

"Joe." Tears filled her eyes. "Someday I hope you learn to see the person I see." Then she got into her car and left.

Chapter Ten

Rose

James was already there waiting, not that I was surprised. He usually beat me.

As soon as I pulled up behind the Sinclair station, he got out of his car and waited for me to climb out.

I offered him a smile, and we walked silently to the back of my truck and put the tailgate down.

"What's with all the mud?" he asked. "Were you carting around plants when the storm hit?"

"No, I carted a pig to the vet."

He gave me a long look. "Do I want to know?"

I laughed. "Probably not." Then I hopped up onto the tailgate.

He lifted a shoulder into a shrug and pulled his flask out of his back pocket before he sat down next me.

I grabbed it from him, unscrewed the cap, then took a swig.

He took it from me and downed his own swig.

We were silent for nearly a minute, staring at the red and pink sky.

"We're going to have to start meeting later if we're going to keep watching the sunset," I said.

"Hey," he said defensively. "The sunset was your idea."

"Yeah," I countered, turning to face him. "Because you said you'd never sat and watched one. I had to remedy that."

"And now I've seen one. I've seen several."

I put my hands behind me and braced myself with stiffened arms. "And you need to see more. You always seem less stressed when you leave."

He smirked. "And you think it's the sunsets that do that?"

I sat up and shoved my shoulder into his arm. "And maybe the company."

He grinned and took another drink.

The truth was I'd been worried about him. Things in the crime world had been tense, and he was struggling to smooth things over with as little violence as possible. But he was still dealing with the fallout of Mick Gentry's attempted coup, as well as some of his underlings questioning his loyalty for helping the sheriff catch J.R. Simmons.

"You still dealing with Wagner's nonsense?" I asked.

"We're not discussing my business."

"We have before. Every time we've met here. What gives?"

He shook his head and took another sip.

"I was in the thick of it last winter, James. What's the point of keeping things from me now?"

"Simmons Jr. is back in town."

I frowned, wondering what that had to do with our conversations. Then it hit me. "You think I'm going to give him information."

He lifted his shoulder in a nonchalant shrug. "Deveraux's gone. Simmons is back."

I snatched the flask from him and threw back a generous gulp. "I expected better from you, James Malcolm," I said, my voice heavy with disappointment.

"You have to understand, Rose, it's not just me I'm thinking about."

"You think I'd tell Joe about our conversations?"

"No, I think Simmons could use our conversations against *you*."

I sighed. "I can take care of Joe."

"Look how well that worked out when he arrested you."

"That was different."

We sat in silence for a moment, each of us mulling over our own thoughts.

"Is he going back to the sheriff's department?" James asked, keeping his gaze on the fiery sky.

"I don't know. I didn't ask him."

"He didn't tell you this afternoon?"

I gaped at him.

He turned to look at me, his face hardening. "Calm down. I had a guy checkin' on him. You just happened to show up."

"I'm not so sure that you checking on the chief deputy sheriff is a good thing."

"The sins of the father, Lady," he said. "He learned at his father's knee. He may have escaped charges, but for all I know, he's angling to take over his father's business. Working in the sheriff's department would be a good way to cover his tracks."

"You really think that's his intention?"

"What if he's preparing to fulfill a personal vendetta against me in retaliation for what I did to his father?"

"Someone has a massive ego," I said dryly. "In case you've forgotten, Joe killed his father. Not you."

"But I helped bring him down."

"So did I, and I'm not worried about either of us."

I was surprised he didn't say that his case was different. I knew it was. He'd lived a life of crime. And Joe wasn't the only one to have learned at J.R. Simmons's knee. J.R. had personally groomed James a long time ago, and Joe knew it.

"I'm not telling Joe or anyone else what we discuss, and if you ever insinuate any differently, I'll kick you in those family jewels you're always so worried about. Got it?"

He chuckled. "Got it."

"Now tell me what's going on with Wagner."

We spent the next half hour discussing his business, mostly the illegal side. His legit businesses seemed to be flourishing. Back in February, he'd told me they were far more profitable than his illegal ones. But he'd also said that if he vacated his role as the crime lord of the county, someone else would take his place. Chances were it would be someone with far fewer scruples.

He was in danger. I knew things had gotten bad, but I hadn't been this worried about him since J.R. Simmons had gotten loose and threatened James's life. The thought of something happening to James filled me with panic.

When he stopped talking, I put my hand on his arm and closed my eyes. I focused on a vision, asking to see our meeting next week.

The vision appeared immediately. I was looking into Vision Rose's face, and she was grinning as she took a sip from the flask.

Satisfied, I ended the vision, a trick I'd learned with practice, yet try as I might, I hadn't figured out a way to stop the next part.

"We're meeting next week."

When I opened my eyes, he was staring into my face with a guarded expression. "You feel reassured now?"

"I'm sorry. I should have asked you first."

His eyes narrowed. "Never be sorry for your visions, Rose."

"It's a violation of your privacy. I was worried, but I still should have asked first."

"Worried?" he asked in surprise. "Worried about me?"

"Of course I'm worried about you. Things are dangerous for you right now, and I hardly hear from you between our meetings. I have no idea if you're okay. Some nights I wake up in the middle of the night in a cold sweat."

"You need to start closing your windows," he teased.

"James."

He looked down at me.

"People keep leaving me," I said in a whisper. "Joe. Mason. Violet. I need you to stay."

He cupped the side of my head and searched my eyes. "Rose, I'm not goin' anywhere. I'm here."

"You can't promise me that."

"And you can't promise me that I'm one hundred percent safe, but if a vision helps you sleep at night, then you have as many visions as you need."

"Thank you," I said past the lump in my throat.

Something flickered in his eyes, and he kissed my forehead. "I need to be heading back," he said, dropping his hand.

"But we still haven't figured out how to handle the Wagner issue."

"You don't need to be figuring it out. That's my job."

"It's always good to have advisors."

"Lady, sometimes just talkin' it over helps."

He hopped off the truck bed, and I followed. "Why don't you talk to Jed?"

"What the hell are you talkin' about? I do talk to Jed."

"Like you do with me?"

He paused. "No."

"Why?"

"Because you're not in the thick of it anymore. And sometimes you just listen without trying to fix things. And because for some reason you don't think I'm weak when I don't have all the answers."

"Jed doesn't think you're weak."

He didn't answer.

"James," I said, a new worry hitting me in the gut. "Has Jed done anything to make you think he's been disloyal?"

I knew Jed. I knew he would lay down his life for Skeeter. He'd also lay down his life for me, and at one point last fall, James had mistaken Jed's allegiance to me as disloyalty until I'd helped him see reason.

"No. But people are turning on me, Lady. I'm getting paranoid."

"Jed is the most loyal friend you could ever have. Don't doubt it." I gave him a small smile. "But sometimes it's good to be able to talk to a friend who's not gonna worry themselves sick over you."

He grinned. "You mean like you?"

"That's different," I protested. "If you stop coming to see me, I'll just hang out at the pool hall until you spill your guts." I cringed. "Wrong choice of words."

He grinned. "Selfishly, I don't want to give up our time together, so I'll keep coming until you tell me you want to stop."

"I don't see that happening for a long time."

"Good." He opened my truck door. "You need to leave first."

I found it amusing that he believed me capable of fending off dangerous criminals, yet he always watched me drive away to make sure I was safe. "I didn't close the tailgate."

"You get in and I'll do it."

"James," I said, turning around to face him. "You can call or text me during the week. If you ever need my help with anything, I'm here for you."

"Thanks. Now climb up in there. I need to get back."

James closed the tailgate, and I waved before backing out and pulling onto the highway. I saw him pull out after me, heading in the opposite direction. As his taillights disappeared in the darkness, an uneasy feeling washed over me. James was still in as much trouble as he'd been in when I showed up in his office last November. I had to wonder how long he had before it all came to a head.

Chapter Eleven
Neely Kate

I parked my car a good twenty feet from Joe's house, my stomach cramping with anxiety. Sure, he'd asked me to come, but he'd asked that I come alone.

That couldn't be a good sign.

I hadn't answered his text. I'd spent a good half hour trying to figure out if I wanted to come at all. He'd ignored me for nearly three months. Was I really expected to drop everything and come running when he called?

Leave it to a dang Simmons to make a request like that.

But in the end, I couldn't stop myself, and that ate at me more than his months of neglect. My mother's words echoed in my head, her laughter as she'd say, "You can always count on Neely Kate to roll over at the mere thought of a belly scratch."

By showing up here, I was proving her right.

I suddenly felt like I was going to throw up.

This was a mistake. Yet I couldn't leave. Tears stung my eyes, blurring the soft glow coming from the living room window.

Go home, Neely Kate. Go home.

But I didn't have a home. Not really. As much as Rose said her house was my home, I couldn't help feeling like I was pretending. Not that it was a struggle. I'd spent my entire life pretending.

And I was so damn tired of it.

The door opened and Joe stepped onto the porch, his hands at his sides. With the light behind him, I couldn't make out much of his face. I gripped the steering wheel, telling myself it wasn't too late to leave. Just because I'd shown up didn't mean I had to go in there and talk to him.

He moved toward the steps and the hair on my neck stood on end. I wasn't sure I could handle more of his rejection.

But then anger rose up, pushing all my fear aside. To hell with Joe Simmons. Why was I sulking like a girl who hadn't been picked for prom? It was his loss, and, by golly, I was going to tell him so.

I got out of the car and slammed the door with more force than necessary.

"You've got a lot of nerve, Joe Simmons!" I shouted as I stomped toward him, my hands fisted at my sides. "You ignored me for three months. Three freaking months!"

He'd made it to the bottom step. I could see his face now, not that it clued me in to what he was thinking. The Simmonses were probably great at poker.

That riled me up even more. "I didn't ask to have that monster as my father! Hell, I didn't ask to have that selfish witch as my mother. But like it or not, that's the hand I was dealt." I shook my head and let out a short laugh. "I never asked for this. I never asked for you to be my half-brother, but here we are. So if you want to pretend like we never found out, then so be it. But it's your damn loss, Joe Simmons."

"Neely Kate."

"No!" I shouted. "I'm not done! I'm sick to death of you Simmonses thinking you're better than everyone else. You think you can make all the rules, and people will just come running whenever you demand it. Well, guess what, Joe? I'm a Simmons too! That's right. I'm just like you. Maybe I didn't grow up in that fancy house and go to college and wear nice clothes, but half my DNA is J.R.'s—just like you." I squared my back, and my nails dug into my palms as I squeezed my hands tighter. "I've spent my whole life feeling like a worthless piece of trash, and I'll be damned if I'll let you make me feel that way too." My voice cracked, and the damn tears were back. "So ignore me if you like, but you're no better than me."

"Neely Kate." His voice sounded ragged as he reached for me and pulled me to his chest, holding me so tight I could barely breathe. "God, I've been so stupid. I'm sorry."

112

To my horror, I started to cry, wrenching sobs that made him shake, but he held tight until I'd sobbed myself out. Then he leaned back and stared into my face. "It's not you, Neely Kate. I've stayed away because I've been ashamed."

"*Ashamed?* Ashamed of *what?*"

"That my father tainted your life. That you've suffered so much because of him. Because you got dragged into this godforsaken mess. That you're linked to all of this . . . to me."

"You mean you're ashamed to be linked to me."

He grasped my shoulders, his fingers digging in as his face hardened. "No. God, no. Don't you ever think that."

"But you ignored—"

"I was an idiot, Neely Kate." He cracked a grin. "Apparently it's a dominant Simmons trait. Thank God it skipped you." His smile fell. "I felt like I failed you— your mother . . . everything you've been through."

"You didn't know." I gasped as a new thought hit me. "Did you know?"

"*No.* I had no clue, but now I can't believe I didn't see it." His grin returned. "There are parts of you that are so Simmons it's scary."

I wiped the tears from my face.

"I'm ashamed that you've been through so much, but you're ten times better than I can ever hope to be." He looked down. "I didn't know what my father was doing, but I should have suspected. I should have investigated."

"Joe, he was your father."

"Apparently he was your father too."

I shook my head, my anger returning. "No. That man wasn't my father. If he had known, he probably would have had me killed."

Tears filled Joe's eyes. "I'm sorry."

I threw my arms around his neck and clung tight. "I'm sorry too. We've both been through our own personal hell. But that's in the past." I dropped my hold on him, suddenly nervous. "It's what we do from here on out that matters."

"What do you want to do from here on out?"

I thought about beating around the bush, but this was too important. I needed to lay it all on the line, even though I was risking my heart. "I want to be part of your life, and I want you to be part of mine. I know DNA really doesn't mean anything. It's about relationships. You and I . . . all we have is bickering and irritating the hell out of each other."

He grinned. "Sounds like siblings to me." When I started to protest, he held up his hand. "We have more than that. We both care about Rose, and I've always cared about you, Neely Kate. I love your spunk and the way you stand up for your friends, even when you turn it against me. And when you miscarried and nearly died, I had to fight my panic to get you to the hospital. Then I didn't leave until I knew you were going to be okay. So it sounds like we're off to a good start." Indecision flickered in his eyes. "But maybe that's not enough."

114

Was he talking about himself or me? My stomach dropped as I bared my soul. "I need you, Joe. And I think you need me too."

A warm smile lit up his face, and a trickle of joy filled my heart. Maybe this could work out. Maybe I'd have a family after all. Sure, it wasn't the family I'd wanted to have with Ronnie, but I'd take what I could get.

As if reading my mind, Joe put his arm around my shoulder and steered me toward the house. "Then as your brother, I need to know what's going on with that idiot husband of yours. Last I heard, he was still missing."

We sat on the porch, and I told him everything—how I felt like I'd cheated Ronnie from having a family because I couldn't have more children. How Ronnie had tried to make me stay away from Rose after her arrest, and how he'd disappeared soon after she was released from jail. And since I was being open, I told him about Ronnie's involvement with J.R. Simmons and Mick Gentry, and how I'd filed for divorce to find him. "But no one can find him, so I'm startin' to think he's dead."

"Who's been looking?" he asked quietly.

"The investigators Carter Hale has hired—all three of them. And—" I stopped.

"And?"

I grimaced. "I found out that someone outside the law has been looking for him too."

"Skeeter Malcolm."

I shot him a look of surprise and concern.

He shrugged, not looking as angry as I'd expected. "It stands to reason that Malcolm would want to squash every part of the rebellion he faced."

"That's not why he's lookin', Joe."

He lifted his eyebrows.

"He's not doing it to punish him. He said he's lookin' for me."

"And you believe him?" he asked, sounding confused.

"Yeah."

He looked unconvinced. "That's not the Malcolm I know. He's ruthless."

"Maybe that's the way he used to be. He's changed."

He sat back in his seat and stared out into the now darkened fields. "Because of Rose."

I didn't answer. I heard the pain in his voice; he knew it was true.

"So Malcolm came up with nothing?"

"Jed agrees that Ronnie's probably dead."

He reached down to the armrest of my chair and covered my hand with his. "Neely Kate, I'm sorry."

"I wasn't going to change my mind about the divorce."

"But you still loved him. You were having a baby with him."

Two babies. But that was a moot point. "And you were having a baby with Hilary." But as soon as the words left my mouth, I regretted them. "Joe. I'm sorry."

He turned to face me. "The Simmons offspring are cursed. All three of us have lost our babies before they were born."

"There's still hope for you." But it was doubtful for me and Kate. Me for obvious reasons; Kate because I suspected she wouldn't get out of the psych ward for a very long time.

"I don't know," he said, stretching out his legs. "I'm not sure it's in the cards for me either. But maybe that's not such a bad thing. Look at the evil my father and Kate did. Maybe it's genetic."

I wasn't sure I believed that, but now didn't seem like the time to debate him.

"Do you really want to find Ronnie?" he asked.

I'd asked myself that question more times than I could count. "Yes. I need closure."

He nodded. "When I go back to the sheriff's department, I'll launch an investigation."

"So you're staying here? You're going back to your job?"

A lopsided grin lifted his mouth. "I just found out about you. We've got about twenty-five years to make up. Besides, as much trouble as you and Rose get into, I can't go leavin' my sister unsupervised."

He looked like a weight had been lifted from his shoulders, and I realized he'd been worried that I wouldn't want him to stick around.

But the mention of Kate brought something else to mind. Something I needed to do.

"Joe, I need a favor. And I need you to do it with me."

He turned to me with an earnest look in his eyes. "Anything, Neely Kate. Name it and I'm there."

I was counting on it.

***

Two days later, I was more nervous than I had expected. Joe stood in front of me in a protective stance, not that I was surprised. Since our conversation two nights before, he'd truly acted like he was making up for lost time. We'd gone out to lunch the next day, and then I'd gone over to his house last night and helped him paint woodwork. This new relationship still felt a little odd, but mostly it felt right. Like something that had been missing had finally lodged into place. And now, as he looked back at me with a worried expression, I was pretty sure he felt it too.

"Are you certain you want to do this?" he asked. "It's not too late to change your mind."

I nodded my head, even if my hands were shaking. "I need to do this. I need to know."

He watched me with a grave look. "Believe it or not, I do too. Thanks for letting me go back with you."

Let him? I needed all the support I could get. But what if he ultimately sided with the sister he'd known most of his life?

A door opened and a woman in scrubs appeared in the doorway. "Mr. and Ms. Simmons?"

I started to correct her, but Joe spoke first. "That's us." Then he put his arm around my lower back, and we walked toward her.

"Your sister is medicated, but she's still prone to rages and delusions. She's liable to lash out and say hateful things. Are you sure you can deal with that?"

Joe looked down at me, his eyes wide with worry. "We don't have to do this now."

"The doctors are still adjusting her meds," the nurse said in an encouraging tone. "She might be more open to a conversation in a few weeks."

Joe's eyes were fixed on me with such intensity that it was like he was willing me to change my mind, but I was ready to face her. Ready to face my demons. I needed to find out what she knew.

I shook my head. "No. I can handle it. Can you?"

He seemed unsure. For a moment, I wondered if I should pretend I wanted to go alone, save him the grief, but he'd already insisted on coming. "You're the strong one between us," he said with a wobbly smile. "I'll follow your lead."

As we followed the nurse down a hall, I thought about Joe's insistence that I was the strong one. I wasn't so sure he was right. It was more likely that we handled things differently.

But I didn't have time to dwell on it. The nurse stopped at the opening of a large recreation room full of about twenty men and women. I expected them to be in hospital gowns, but they were all in street clothes. I spotted Kate in the corner wearing a pair of yoga pants and a T-shirt. Her hair was longer—almost to her shoulders—and her streaks had grown out too.

"Is she expecting us?" Joe asked.

"Yes," the nurse said. "Her reaction was part of the reason I wanted to warn you. While she seemed happy, she also seemed like she was up to something . . . devious."

Joe looked down at me. "It's not too late to change your mind."

"We already drove all this way. I'm not afraid of her." And I wasn't—not of *her*. But I *was* afraid of what she might tell me, not that I was going to admit that to Joe.

"Just say the word and we're gone."

I cocked my head. "But you want to talk to her too."

"Whatever I have to say can wait." His gaze held mine. "We need to stick together in this. If you need to go, we go."

"And you too," I said, sneaking a glance toward Kate.

She'd noticed us, and a cagey grin lit up her face.

He nodded and the nurse led us across the room until we reached her. Kate sat in a chair with a half-completed jigsaw puzzle of a barn in front of her.

She grinned, her gaze roving over us. "If I'd known you were coming, I would have dressed up."

I bit back a retort that she was more dressed up than I usually saw her; I wanted my answers. No sense starting off by antagonizing her. I suspected it would escalate quickly enough.

She waved to the three chairs surrounding her square table. "Have a seat."

Joe sat down, and I pulled out a chair, trying not to cringe as the wood scraped the linoleum floor.

"Now, Kate," the nurse said, "be nice, or your brother and sister will have to leave before your visit is up."

That brought a smile to her lips, but she looked up at the nurse and held her straightened index and middle finger to her temple before swinging them out in a mock salute. "Yes, ma'am."

The nurse watched her for a moment, clearly not trusting her.

Smart woman. I didn't trust Kate either.

Kate leaned forward, placing her hands flat on the tabletop. "No one told me it was family day. Mom didn't want to come?" Her voice rose, carrying over the entire room. "Of course, Dad couldn't make it—seeing as how you shot him in the head and killed him."

Joe flinched, but he gave her a nearly expressionless look. Neither of us said anything. Kate was volatile and I was terrified of setting her off before I got what I needed from her.

"So . . ." Kate said, leaning back and crossing her legs. "I see you two are besties now." She turned her gaze to Joe and narrowed her eyes. "But then, you always were trying to replace me. Look at Hilary. You two left me out. For some reason, I was never good enough."

Guilt clouded Joe's eyes, but his voice was firm. "Kate, that's not true or fair. We were kids. You and I weren't supposed to get along. Especially in *that* house. But I tried after you moved to Little Rock. I wanted to have a relationship with you. I reached out to you multiple times."

"Whenever it fit into your schedule," she sneered.

Joe started to protest, but his shoulders settled and he looked beaten down. "I was an asshole, Kate. I'm sorry."

She started to laugh. "I'm sorry. I'm not sure I heard you correctly. What did you say?"

I expected him to get angry, but this was a different Joe than the one I'd known for months. He just looked devastated. "I'm sorry, Kate. You have no idea how sorry I am."

That seemed to appease her. She nodded and turned to me. "I'm surprised to see you here, *sis*."

I forced a smile. "I always wanted a sister, but you could have found a better way to tell me. Your timing kind of sucked. I have enough drama in my life without you adding to it."

Kate grinned. "I've always liked you. You've got spunk. That's part of the reason I was sure you were a Simmons. I have no idea why you waste your time with that milquetoast Rose."

I chose to ignore her statement about Rose, instead focusing on her previous interest in me. She'd always shown more interest in me than made sense. "How did you figure it out?"

"Is that why you're here?" she asked with guarded eyes.

I had to answer carefully. "It's part of it. Something had to tip you off."

"I was trying to figure out dear ol' Dad's obsession with Fenton County. I made the connection to Skeeter Malcolm, and then I realized Rose's birth mother was connected to the factory, and the whole meal got extra delicious. But something about *you* just piqued my interest," Kate said, staring into my eyes. "And knowing our father's penchant for young girlfriends and your current age, well, the timing all seemed to work. At first I thought it might have been Rose—wouldn't that have been quite *scandalous*, Joe sleeping with his half-sister?"

Joe cringed but didn't say anything.

Kate's eyes lit up when she saw his reaction, but she let it go. "But after I did a little digging, I figured out who Daddy Dearest's girlfriend actually was. The trick was tracking her down. But once I did, the rest was easy."

"So you found her?" I asked, trying not to sound eager. "Where was she?"

"Poor Neely Kate," she said with fake sympathy. "Somebody has mommy issues."

"Kate," Joe said, "you went to so much trouble to prove that Neely Kate is our sister. Why not tell us both what you found?"

Kate continued to watch me. "Did you have a DNA test done?"

"No."

She tsked and pretended to look at her nail beds. "You can't get your hands on all that money if you don't prove you're part of the family."

"Then you don't know me very well," I said in a harsh tone. "Because I don't want it."

"Kate," Joe said quietly. "There's no more money."

She scrunched her nose in irritation. "Yeah, right. I bet Mom siphoned a lot off, but I know for a fact you and I have trusts. She can't touch that."

"No. It's gone. All of it. The house too. The FBI took it all."

Her eyes widened and her mouth dropped. "What?"

"All of Dad's cronies caved and turned on one another and him. His house of cards was built on fraud and extortion. Some of the money came from his law practice, but good luck untangling it all."

"So where's Mom?"

"With her parents."

For once, all of Kate's pretense fell away, leaving her exposed and vulnerable. That was the woman I could feel sympathy for. Not the woman who had orchestrated a plot to kill us all three months ago. Then again, I wasn't sure that had actually been her plan.

"Why did you want me at the warehouse?" I asked.

Her eyes flicked up to me in surprise. Then her façade slid back into place like a tight-fitting glove. "I didn't want you to miss all the fun."

"Kate," I said quietly. "*Why?*"

"To hurt my father—*our* father. He'd been so untouchable for so many years. I wanted him to suffer—to see that he wasn't in control of the situation. I wanted to see him vulnerable and scared."

"Except, it didn't work out that way," Joe said with an edge to his voice. "He was never scared, and he never acted vulnerable. In fact, it was just the opposite."

She glanced away.

"Why was Mason there?" I asked.

Her gaze jerked back to me, her eyes hard. "Did Rose Petal put you up to that one?"

"No. I'm asking out of curiosity."

"I've heard that Mason left Rose." She turned to Joe and gave him a sly grin. "Which means she's available."

"Oh, my God, Kate," Joe groaned. "*Stop.* Just stop."

Disappointment flickered in her eyes before she turned her attention to me. "I wanted Rose to watch when I killed him. I wanted to see her suffer."

"Why? She never did anything to you."

She shrugged indifferently. "Why not?" But I could see she was holding something back. "But that's not why you're here, is it? You want to know about your momma. Do you want me to tell you?"

"That depends," I said. "Are you actually going to tell me, or do you plan on wastin' our time?"

Kate lifted her eyebrows and looked offended. "Hey, I didn't ask you to come. You'll take what you get, and you won't throw a fit. Don't they teach that back in Podunk Fenton County? But then, you didn't always live there, did you? Joe and I learned that rule in our expensive private school—not that it ever really applied to us—while you were in Ardmore, Oklahoma, living in a trailer with your momma and her loser boyfriend of the week. Who knows," she said with a sneer, "maybe it was the loser your momma let sleep with you."

My heart jolted and I thought I was going to pass out. Had my mother told her that?

"Kate." Joe's voice was hard and authoritative. "*Enough.*"

"What?" Kate asked in mock innocence. "She wanted answers. I'm just trying to prove I'm a credible source." She turned to me with a saccharine smile. "How'm I doing?"

I stuffed down my shock and told myself I could lose it later. She was right. I wanted answers, but I was going to have to pay for them. Rose and I had already figured out that quirk months ago.

"Something like that is bound to mess a girl up," she said, pursing her lips into a mock pout. "But enough about that nonsense. You want me to tell you that your momma is pining for you. That she regrets it all and wakes up every day wishing she hadn't dropped you off at your granny's front door like a load of trash at the county dump. Isn't that why you're here?"

She was trying to make me run, but I dug in my heels and kept my face neutral, no matter how much I wanted to cry. "I just want the truth, Kate. I thought that's why you found her. You were lookin' for the truth. You owe it to Joe and me to tell us what you know."

Kate narrowed her eyes and pointed her finger at me. "Let's get one thing straight, Neely *Kate*. I'm making the rules here." Then she sat up and grinned. "I bet you didn't know you were partially named after me, did you? Your momma knew all about me, so she tagged you with my name."

"Kate. Enough." Joe sighed. "What did you find out?"

"I think you know the details. Asshole impregnates teen. Teen runs away. Teen turns to life of drugs, booze, and trailer trash living. Baby grows up and becomes a thorn in the former teen's love life." She cocked her head. "Nothing like your preteen daughter catchin' the eye of your man. So Neely Kate had to go."

She wasn't telling me anything I hadn't already suspected, but my heart still felt like it was being sliced to ribbons.

"You need to leave that woman in the past, Neely Kate," she said, doing a piss-poor job of pretending to be sympathetic. "*We're* your family now. You're a Simmons. But then, you acted like one before you even knew the truth."

"I'm nothing like you," I spat out, dangerously close to tears.

"Don't be so sure about that. What happened in those two years you took off and left Fenton County?"

I sucked in my breath. What did she know? "That's none of your business, Kate. It has *nothin'* to do with any of this."

"Are you sure?" she asked, her eyebrows rising high enough to be hidden behind her bangs.

"Kate," Joe said, sounding exasperated. "Neely Kate's right. It has nothing to do with this. Tell her about her mother."

"There's nothing much to tell. I found her in West Virginia, although she didn't look much like her old photos. She's missing a few teeth, and her hair's thinned out. All that hard livin', I suppose." She gave me a grin. "Good thing you got the Simmons genes in the looks department."

I couldn't bring myself to respond. I was trying to remember what my mother looked like the last time I'd seen her. Other than the photos Granny had of her growing up, I didn't have a single photo of her—let alone of her and me—and she wasn't on any social media. I checked every few weeks or so.

"She confirmed everything I had already deduced," Kate said. "But, funny thing, she never once asked about how you were doin' or what you were up to. I tried to tell her all about you, but she couldn't be bothered."

I tried to control my breathing while Joe put his hand on mine and turned his wrath on our sister. "You having fun, Kate?"

"Yeah," she said with a wide smile. "Actually, I am." She tilted her head, her eyes on me, watching me like a hawk. "I offered to show her a photo of you."

"Because you just happened to have one?" I asked in a snotty tone. "Stalker much?"

"You have no idea the lengths I'll go to when I want to find something. Then again, maybe you do. You and Rose know from when you broke into my apartment." She smirked. "See? I told you that you're a Simmons. But I've got years on you, sis, and I'm very good at getting what I want."

"Oh, my God," I gasped. "You're sick."

Kate started laughing hysterically, catching the attention of the nurse who'd brought us back. As if sensing the nurse was about to intervene, Kate settled down. "Your mother doesn't want you, Neely Kate. Isn't that why you're really here? Not to see me. Not for confirmation that what I've said is true. You know it is. You both do. What you're really here for is for me to tell you that your mother regrets leaving you. But guess what? She doesn't. She's happy she abandoned you and wishes you were never born. She blames you for screwin' up her life. Every single bad thing that happened to her was after you took root in her uterus like a parasite." She smiled. "I can confirm it all. She doesn't even want to hear your name."

Joe's face turned red and he got to his feet. "Neely Kate, we're done here."

I looked up at him blankly, lost in my own head as Kate's words confirmed my nightmare.

"Aww . . ." Kate cooed, looking up at Joe in adoration. "Isn't that sweet. You're already acting like a protective big brother."

"Shut up, Kate," he said, grabbing my arm and pulling me to my feet. "Our father may have been a monster, but that's no excuse for what you're doing now."

"You two deserve each other," she said, but Joe was pulling me across the room and down the hall. The nurse stopped him to ask about our conversation. Joe answered her with a few short sentences before he dragged me out of the hospital and into his car.

We both sat in silence, and I watched the magnolia blossoms on a nearby tree sway in the breeze. This felt surreal.

"Neely Kate."

I shook my head. "Don't."

"She's a pathological liar."

I turned to him. "Is she? If she is, how do we pick and choose what to believe? Maybe J.R. isn't my biological father after all."

"He is."

"How can you be sure?" Then it hit me and disappointment washed over me. "You had me tested. That's why you didn't answer me for months. You were waiting for the results."

"Neely Kate," he said, his voice ragged. "I knew you were my half-sister before I even left Fenton County. I had you tested right away, but I did it for your protection, not mine. I stopped by Rose's house while she was in the hospital and got your hairbrush. I know Kate's a liar, and I didn't want you hurt any more than you already were."

"By ignoring me?" I asked in disbelief.

"Believe it or not, I was ignoring you to protect you too. From my mother. From the press. From the absolute mess that was going on with the FBI. They didn't know you existed, and I wanted to keep it that way. But it was also from the shame of having failed you. I felt like you deserved better, and I didn't deserve to have you in my life. So as stupid as it sounds now, staying away from you felt like the right thing to do. It was the only way I knew to protect you. I'm so very sorry I hurt you, Neely Kate." He looked close to breaking down. "But I'm mostly sorry that my sorry excuse for a family continues to hurt you."

I searched his face and saw that he was telling me the truth.

"What Kate said about your mother. God, Neely Kate." I heard the anguish in his voice. "Your mother . . . I can't believe it. Is it true?"

I fought to hold back my tears. "Joe. I can't talk about her. Or what she did."

"It's okay. I'm sorry." His voice broke. Then he cupped the side of my head and turned me to face him.

"I will do everything in my power to make this right for you."

I shook my head. "This isn't your doing."

"I know," he said with a grin even though his eyes glistened with tears. "But isn't that a big brother's job?"

I started to cry, and he pulled my head to his shoulder, rubbing my back in slow circles.

"I swear to God, Neely Kate, I'll make this up to you. I'll never leave you to fend for yourself again."

I leaned back and stared at him in amazement. "You can't promise such a thing."

"I think I just did."

"*Joe.*"

He took a deep breath and sat back in his seat, looking serious. "Since you've never had a big brother before, I think it's time I fill you in on what the duties entail, and then we'll move on to your duties as my sister."

I laughed, wiping the tears from my cheeks. "Why do I have a feeling *my* duties will be heinous and include making sure you get home-cooked meals every once in a while?"

He shook his head. "No need to worry about the home-cooked meals. Maeve seems to have that covered, but there are other duties, which include but are not limited to making sure I don't screw up my laundry—and occasionally cleaning my house."

"That has to be the most sexist statement I've ever heard you say," I protested, but his grin told me he was teasing. "So what do I get out of this deal?"

"You get to bask in my stellar company. What more could you possibly want?"

I laughed, amazed that I could go from such devastation to elation within a matter of moments. And although he was right—the only thing I wanted from him was him—I wasn't about to let him off that easy. "I think this means that you have to come kill any spiders I find in my house."

"You've got to be kidding," he said as he pulled out of the parking lot. "Now *that's* a sexist statement, not to mention you of all people should know you shouldn't kill spiders."

"What makes you think I would know that?" I demanded.

"You work for a landscaping business. Aren't you supposed to protect spiders so they kill other insects?"

"My motto is the only good spider is a dead one, but don't think I didn't notice that you changed the subject. I think we need to spend more time discussing your duties as my brother."

He flashed a grin, and I reveled in the fact that Joe Simmons and I were not only in a car together, but family. Kate had done a lot of bad things, but this was one thing she'd gotten right.

Still, I couldn't forget the look on Kate's face as Joe dragged me away.

And I knew for a fact she wasn't done with us yet.

About the Author

N ew York Times and *USA Today* bestselling author Denise Grover Swank was born in Kansas City, Missouri and lived in the area until she was nineteen. Then she became a nomadic gypsy, living in five cities, four states and ten houses over the course of ten years before she moved back to her roots. She speaks English and smattering of Spanish and Chinese which she learned through an intensive Nick Jr. immersion period. Her hobbies include witty Facebook comments (in her own mind) and dancing in her kitchen with her children. (Quite badly if you believe her offspring.) Hidden talents include the gift of justification and the ability to drink massive amounts of caffeine and still fall asleep within two minutes. Her lack of the sense of smell allows her to perform many unspeakable tasks. She has six children and hasn't lost her sanity. Or so she leads you to believe.

You can find out more about Denise and her other books at www.denisegroverswank.com

Don't miss out on Denise's newest releases! Join her mailing list: http://denisegroverswank.com/mailing-list/